DATE D

W9-BAJ-153

AN AVALON HISTORICAL ROMANCE

ABSOLUTION
A Love's Valley Historical Romance

Carolyn Brown

The Irish are hardheaded so Elspeth Hamilton doesn't like them. The Mexicans are hotheaded so likewise, she doesn't think much of them either. Since Rebels burned her family home, killing both her parents in the Chambersburg, Pennsylvania fire, it stands to reason she surely doesn't waste affection on Rebels. Colum Sullivan is all three: Irish, Mexican, and Rebel. It would take an utter absence of sanity and total absolution of all the past to fall in love with Colum.

The English are a stiff-necked lot so Colum doesn't like Ellie. The Yankees are a coldblooded bunch so likewise he doesn't like her. All he's going to do is rescue her and then light a shuck back to Texas. But an early blizzard in the mountains of southern Pennsylvania turns his plans around abruptly. Colum admires the lady but that's as far as it's going because it's absolutely the wrong time in the century for the likes of a lady like Ellie Hamilton and a man like Colum Sullivan to get together. Those kinds of miracles only happen once in a lifetime, and his sister Douglass and her new husband Monroe have already captured that miracle.

ABSOLUTION

•

Carolyn Brown

AVALON BOOKS

NEW YORK

PRINTED IN THE UNITED STATES OF AMERICA
ON ACID-FREE PAPER
BY HADDON CRAFTSMEN, BLOOMSBURG, PENNSYLVANIA

With love
to my mother,
Virginia Essary

Chapter One

Ellie Hamilton glared through a swollen, black and blue eye with pure, unadulterated hatred at the man holding her captive. There was one advantage to having the other eye completely swollen shut. It shielded her from having to view the whole despicable kidnapper.

"Why are you doing this? Monroe would have paid you the money," she whispered hoarsely.

"The great Monroe Hamilton paid only half of what we wanted. He left a note with the money and said we'd get the other half when you was brought home. Now that's a big joke, ain't it? We let you go, we ain't never seein' no more money anyway," the big man who'd introduced himself as Turley, spit a stream of tobacco juice right at her feet. "Way I figure it, is he paid half the money. He can have half the woman. He can have your dead body if he finds it before the wolves and bears come 'round."

She turned her head and clamped her mouth shut in a firm line. Death would be a blessing after the past week. The man was right about Monroe having nothing but her dead body. At the rate the fever was rising, it wouldn't be long until she'd draw her last breath. Her chest hurt every time she inhaled so pneumonia had probably already set in and

1

few people survived that dreaded malady. A bullet would surely be a blessing compared to what would happen to her if he left her in the filthy cabin with no water or food for another day.

"Shoot me, then." Her mouth was dry and raspy.

"Why would I do that? You'll be dead in a couple of days. No Ellie, I won't shoot you. I'm going to leave you here to freeze to death." He laughed. "Your rich cousin Monroe should have paid the whole bundle, then he would've gotten the whole woman. Hell, he barely paid enough to get your memories."

Ellie didn't strain against the iron shackles around both her ankles. She'd tried that when she'd regained consciousness. She'd even tried in vain to pick the locks with a hairpin. She'd been humiliated and was nigh unto death but she wasn't dead yet and if she beat the grim reaper out of a soul, she fully well intended to tear those horrible men into little bitty pieces and feed them to the hogs.

"Don't you sit there acting like some kind of English royalty," the man said from the doorway. "You're just plain ugly. An old maid that ain't even worth the price Monroe did pay for you. You'll be doin' the world a favor when you die."

She raised her chin and looked down her nose at him, feverish blue eyes glistening in amusement. If she was English royalty then he was the offspring of an illegitimate pirate and a pig farmer's half-witted daughter. Her face split into a wide smile at the vision of him living in a pigsty with a one-eyed father kicking him around with a wooden leg. Anything to keep her mind off of freezing to death on the outside and burning up with fever on the inside.

"Don't you look down on me like that," he yelled and kicked her in the thigh at the same time.

She grabbed his leg and laughed hysterically when he fell hard on his backside on the dirty wooden floor. "I'll look at you anyway I want," she whispered into his ear as he gasped, trying to refill his lungs with air. "I *am* English royalty compared to you."

He slapped her again across the other cheek and bounced up onto his feet. "Time to go," he said to someone outside the door. "They'll find her bones next spring if she's lucky. If not, maybe the wolves or a nice big bear will take care of even that. Leave the door open. Invite the bears and wolves to come right in for a tasty supper. It's already warmed with fever and waiting."

Laughter filled the icy mountain air followed by the pounding of horse hooves as the men left her to either freeze to death or die from pneumonia. They'd only netted half of their demands for ransom, but there were other swindles up their sleeves, and the day was young.

A rush of cold air brought on a chill that rattled Ellie's bones. A rat slithered out from under one of the cots and eyed her. She was aware of the dried blood in her blond hair and shuttered at the thought of that varmint smelling it. With beady little eyes staring right at her, it crept across the floor sniffing the air, already salivating at the idea of something to feast upon. Ellie shuddered again and threw the chamber pot at the rat. What did it matter anyway? She was going to be dead before she needed to use the pot again. The rat investigated the broken porcelain chards and Ellie screamed, hoping to scare it out the open door. She scrunched up in a ball in the corner. The chains attached to the shackles on her ankles went through a hole in the wall to the outside where she figured they were latched firmly into a tree or a log. They were cold against her bare arm but she didn't have time to think about that. Not with a rat the size of a mountain lion about to attack her. She'd have to grab it by the neck and squeeze the life from it before it bit her or she could end up with more than just pneumonia.

"Well, come on rat," she whispered. "I might be weak and seeing two of you at times, but I'm still bigger than you."

The rat kept coming closer and closer, then suddenly a movement near the front door caught Ellie's attention. Monroe had come to rescue her at last, she thought, as she jerked her head in that direction, ignoring the rat. Monroe was her cousin, just married to Douglass Sullivan last week. Relief washed over her. He'd take her home to Love's Valley and call the doctor.

It wasn't Monroe.

A lanky yellow and white cat eased through the door, made a chortling sound deep in her throat and lunged toward the rat who was so intent on finding the blood odor that it forgot to run. The cat seized it by the throat, ignored the flip-ping and flopping of the skinny body as it fought against death, and trotted outside the shack to feed a litter of hungry kittens born late in the fall.

Cold tears ran down Ellie's hot cheeks as she watched the mother cat carry her prey outside. A hungry rat just stalked her and she'd been saved by a yellow cat, but the cat couldn't save her from a big black bear coming in for its last meal before hibernation. Or even a pack of wolves intent upon supper.

Ellie shut her eyes and envisioned that day a week ago when she'd been so distraught, the last time she'd seen her Aunt Laura, her cousins, Monroe, and Indigo. She'd stood on the balcony in her Aunt Laura's house in Love's Valley, Pennsylvania, and sobbed her heart out. She didn't think anything could be worse than what she'd just endured.

She was to play the piano for Monroe and Douglass' wed-ding. But she'd been in the wrong place at the wrong time just outside the house when she overheard Oscar, her fiancé, telling some fellow that as soon as he was married and had control of Ellie's money he would be leaving Love's Valley. Ellie could stay or go. He really didn't care. All he was interested in was the money anyway. A few minutes later, Douglass had caught her crying on the balcony and she'd admitted to her soon-to-be-cousin-in-law that she couldn't marry the man. Yet, she had to or else suffer shame. In the end, just before she went downstairs to play the piano, she'd promised Douglass she would break off the engagement right after the wedding.

And she did. Oscar had sworn at her, telling her that she wasn't anything but an old maid and was lucky to have him, but she'd held her head high and told that rascal just what she thought of him, threw his ring back in his face, and walked right back into the house. It was late and everyone had already retired, but she hadn't been able to sleep. When the first rays of dawn came she put on her work dress and boots and went to muck out horse stalls. Anything to keep her hands busy and her mind off the man who'd almost duped her. She had walked into the barn, felt a presence behind her and woke up chained to the cabin wall.

It seemed like years ago, but in reality couldn't have been more than a week ago. The men came every day to bring bread and fresh water, but only enough to drink. There was dried blood in her long, blond hair from where one of them had hit her with the butt of a pistol. Two of them: Turley, the one who used the trapper's cabin in the winter from what she could piece together of their conversations, and the other one, with tobacco stained teeth, thinning yellow hair and a big belly that hung over his belt. They called him Alvie and he made Ellie's skin crawl, the way he looked at her with his beady little eyes. Come to think of it, those eyes weren't totally unlike the rat's eyes. Maybe they'd shared the same father.

Where was Monroe?

"Lord, where is Monroe? Please send him before I die," Ellie whispered through a parched throat. She'd give anything for a drink of cool water from the well at the back of the house in Love's Valley. Or even a cup of stale water from the bucket Turley, or was it Alvie, had set beside her during those long nights when she was left alone in the cold cabin. But he'd kicked it over when she fought with him. Vengeance had its rewards, but it also had its penalties.

Bracing herself on the wall, she stood to her feet and took two staggering steps forward so she could see out the door. Fog still lay thick upon the ground and the air had an icy bite to it that said winter was setting in. There would be an early snow this year. Ellie could smell it, and with it would be hungry predators. Everything began to spin as she looked out the door. The fog got denser and denser and what little light there was became darker and darker until she fell into a heap of bloody blond hair and weak bones encased in a tattered and torn dirty dress.

Where are you Monroe? They aren't going to bring me home. Come and rescue me, please, Monroe. Come and take me home.

It was her last thought before unconsciousness claimed her tortured body.

Colum Sullivan pulled his .44 caliber Colt Walker from the holster on the side of his saddle, aimed carefully so that one bullet would do the job, and with a steady hand, killed his horse. The luck of the Irish certainly wasn't riding with him that cold, foggy morning. He had been fortunate since he started following the men who'd picked up the saddle-bags with Monroe's money. They hadn't even tried to hide their tracks so he couldn't complain too badly, but faith and begora, now he was on foot out here in hostile territory.

'Twas a pretty country if a man liked mountains, which Colum didn't. He'd learned that the mountain on his left was Blacklog, hence the name of the valley where he rode. The one on his right was Shade Mountain and the other side of it lay Shade Valley. There was one stretch after another of mountains and little narrow valleys in between. Blacklog Valley seemed to be a little bit wider than Love's Valley which was just over the mountains to his left. A stream ran parallel to the road and Colum had drank from it several times during the past couple of days. But Colum didn't like the closed-in feeling the mountains evoked in him. Give him the flat lands of Texas any day over this unforgiving place where winter pushed fall out too early.

He'd promised himself that if he ever got out of the Virginia mountains and back to Texas after the war ended, he'd never look at anything bigger than the gentle rolling hills of north Texas again. The promise had lasted a year. Until his baby sister, Douglass Esmerelda, ran away with that good-for-nothing newspaper man, Raymond Pierce. At least she'd realized her mistake early on and hadn't actually married the worthless, smooth-talking fool.

Colum pulled the hand-tooled saddle and bedroll from the dead horse, slung it over his shoulder and commenced walking. It wasn't more than a mile or two farther. *Of all the blasted luck anyway.* Almost to the place and his horse had stepped into a hole, falling forward and sending Colum to land face first in the cold dirt. One look was all it took to see the horse's leg bone protruding from the skin. There was nothing to do but put it out of misery and keep going on foot.

Douglass Esmerelda was going to owe him big time for this. By now he should be more than halfway back to Texas with his younger brother, Flannon. Not tracking down some bad man who'd kidnapped Ellie, that shrew of a woman— cousin to Douglass's new husband, Monroe. But of all six brothers, Colum was the one who had the softest heart when it came to his younger sister.

"Colum, you've got to track them. They aren't going to bring her home. She's seen them. They'll kill her, Colum. I know it in the bottom of my heart," she'd said, wiping tears the whole time.

Colum had capitulated immediately.

Right then as he trudged along, heavy, fully loaded saddle on one shoulder and a chip on the other because he was tracking a woman he thoroughly disliked, he wished he had escaped from Love's Valley the morning after the wedding. Before they'd found Ellie missing. He could have been far enough away that Douglass couldn't possibly call him back to track the kidnappers. From the nip in the air and the gray clouds he'd be willing to bet there was snow on the wind and to a man on foot that meant sitting down and waiting it out. Colum did not look forward to any of it. He yearned for Texas with its fall leaves this time of year and just the hint of coolness in the morning air.

"Well, little sister, you'd better hope that's not snow I smell in the air because if I can't get home to Texas before winter sets in this forsaken Yankee place, I'm going to be an old bear to live with. And I'm going to take it all out on you," he said, shifting the saddle to a more comfortable position as he walked. "And I may shoot Patrick when I get home for bringin' Raymond home with him. That's what started this whole mess," he declared vehemently as he stomped along the road.

Dead horse behind him.

Snow in front of him.

A gut full of anger inside him.

Anger at his sister for uprooting his life even if he did love her. She didn't have to fall for that smooth-talking Yank's lies, did she? Raymond had told her he loved her and let her believe they were eloping. Only when they'd gotten a day's journey from DeKalb, Texas and her reputation was in shambles, he'd informed her he only wanted a play toy to keep his bed warm on the way back to Philadelphia. That's when she made the choice to get out of the stagecoach and sit in the middle of the road on her trunk. And that's when Monroe Hamilton happened by on his way home to Love's Valley, Pennsylvania from south Texas. A Yankee soldier sent to Galveston to help in the rebuilding process following the war, he had been a gentleman and believed Douglass's lies when she told him she was on her way to Philadelphia to visit an aunt. Douglass surely wasn't stupid and she knew she needed to put space between her brothers' rage and her own future, which she figured was going to be kneeling most of the day in a convent for her foolishness in disgracing two old family names.

Colum and Flannon were sent to bring Douglass home and/or kill Raymond Pierce. If they weren't married, then Michael Sullivan's orders were to make him wish he'd never messed around with the baby girl of the Sullivan family. Colum had actually looked forward to giving Raymond a thrashing. At least the first couple of days. After that, he would have rather flogged Douglass for leading him on a merry chase all the way across the countryside. By the time they found her in Love's Valley, she and Monroe had fallen in love and were married the next week.

"Lord have mercy on that man's poor soul," Colum mumbled to himself as he kept plodding along. "I wouldn't wish Douglass Esmerelda on my worst enemy, not even a Yank. He's got a hard row to hoe cut out for him."

Colum had been the best of the best when it came to tracking for the Confederate Army. They said he could smell the enemy a mile away; said he could track a bumble bee in a snowstorm. But mostly he'd just been acutely aware of his surroundings.

Like right then when his raven black hair stood straight up on his neck and arms. He narrowed his light brown, pecan-colored eyes, and tilted his head to one side. Suddenly, he felt a tingling through the soles of his boots and stopped in his tracks, every sense intensified as he waited. He heard laughter floating through the fog. More than one man and horses or pack mules were riding at an angle, then turned away from him. The last contact he had with a real person back in a town called Orbisonia said a fellow named Turley had just left his general store. Had bought a loaf of bread every day for the past week. Seemed odd because Turley usually stocked up on supplies and then didn't surface again until spring when he holed up in his cabin for the winter.

"Where is this cabin and what's he do?" Colum asked.

"He traps back at the base of Blacklog Valley" the store owner had said. "That Turley is a mean man and he runs with another just like him. Goes by the name of Alvie. Don't just go waltzing in there. They'll rob you blind and then leave you to die."

"Just two of them?" Colum asked.

"Sometimes. Sometimes there's three. Sometimes a whole gang of them. But Turley's been runnin' alone lately. Mighta left the others at the camp though. I'd be right careful if I was tryin' to draw him out. Could be there'd be a bunch of them in the cabin. Hey, you got a strange sound to your voice. Where you from?" the store owner asked.

"Texas, sir," Colum answered.

"You're a rebel, ain't you?"

"Yes, sir, I fought on the side of the Confederacy," Colum nodded truthfully.

"Any kin to that rebel Monroe Hamilton brought home? I heared she was from Texas," the man had set his jaw in a firm line.

"My sister," Colum said.

"Well, we don't take to mixed marriages in these parts, son. I expect you'd better get on your horse and get on back to Texas where you belong," he'd said seriously.

Nothing I want more, Colum thought, standing there in the middle of the road, listening to the sound of men's laughter, and feeling the sound of their horses' hooves under his feet. So much for catching them and finding out where they'd stashed Ellie, if indeed they had her anywhere. Colum sighed. Hopefully there was an empty trapper's cabin not too far ahead. Tomorrow morning he'd commence the walk back through Blacklog Valley to Orbisonia. At least there was a stage there going to Shirleysburg. He could rent a buggy to take him back into Love's Valley to tell his sister and her new family that he hadn't found Ellie.

The cabin rose up through the fog like an apparition. Only a few shades darker than the dense gray fog itself, it appeared to sit in clouds of mist. The door swung open but nothing moved in or around the place. Colum dropped his saddle behind a dead fall, untied the leather binding on the Colt pistol he wore on his hip and waited. Rushing wasn't his style. If it had been he would have been a dead man long ago. Wait and see was his motto.

Someone was screaming hysterically, but he couldn't tell if the screams were from a hysterical woman or a man with a high-pitched voice. Something about going out the door and getting away, but Colum wasn't taking unnecessary chances. It might be Ellie but then it might be one of those drunk trappers mad at the other men for leaving him behind.

He watched a yellow and white cat sneak upon the cabin, then in moments it came out toting a rat. The cat carried the prey up under the house. Then a shadow passed near the front door. Whoever was in the house didn't come right up to the door, but paused back a little way. A thud let him know that the person either dropped something or fell.

Then all was silent. Still Colum waited. Finally, after half an hour he palmed his pistol and eased his way toward the shack. He heard kittens growling and hissing under the porch but nothing else. He stepped out from behind the last tree in full view of anyone who might be peeping out through the one window. Nothing happened so he rushed inside the open door, spinning in a hundred and eighty degree circle, adrenaline pulsating the veins in his head.

Still nothing.

Until something brushed against the leg of his trousers. He looked down expecting to see another cat or perhaps a rat scurrying across the nasty floor. "Faith and begora," he muttered when it registered that he was looking at Ellie Hamilton, crumbled in an awkward position with both legs shackled into irons attached to chains that ran through a hole out the back of the cabin.

He laid two fingers on her neck. There was a pulse but it wasn't anything to brag about, and the fever in her body burned his hands. He stuck his pistol back in the holster and ran outside to his saddle.

It only took a minute to find the little tool pack in his saddlebags but it took almost ten minutes for his clammy hands to tumble the locks open on the leg irons. He'd foiled locks just like those many times in less than three minutes when he needed to release a Confederate soldier, but great glory, it had been almost a year since he'd had to use the picks. When the shackles were loose, he checked Ellie's pulse again and she was still alive. He picked her up ever so gently and carried her to the cot shoved up against the wall. The straw mattress was filthy but it wasn't as bad as the floor.

"Monroe," she mumbled through cracked, swollen lips. "So sorry."

"Lady," he said, grabbing a bucket and heading out the back door toward the little creek running behind the shack, mumbling to himself the whole way, "you don't look like much right now and you might die before mornin' ends. But the sorry man who did this better hope and pray that you live and he's stone cold dead when I find him. You might be an uppity Yank who thinks she's some kind of royalty, but in the south we string up men who do things like this to womenfolk and I'm a southern man. He'll wish he was dead and the devil will have his soul tied up with a pretty bow before I finish with him."

Chapter Two

The first flakes of snow floated softly down from pale gray skies just as Colum carried the pail of water through the back door to the cabin. The primary order of business was to get some liquid into Ellie. She'd lose body fluids rapidly with a fever that high. He found a tin cup behind a cloud of dust on one of the shelves lining the walls, washed it out and filled it with clear, cold water.

"Now, you got to drink," he said softly as he raised her head, but she didn't rouse, not even when he put the cup to her lips and tilted it. All of it ran down the front of her badly soiled dress. "Okay," he sighed, "guess that ain't goin' to work. Maybe you need rest or maybe you are dying already and your throat is shut off."

He set the cup beside the bed and stood to his feet. The cabin was barely twelve foot square. Shelves hung by rusty nails into the weathered wood walls held a few supplies, but not enough to carry a trapper through the winter. Dust and filth were everywhere. Colum turned around three times in the center of the room. Two cots. One where Ellie lay dying. One shoved against the other wall. Both strung with frayed rope that wouldn't hold his body weight. One straw-filled tick filled with holes and smelling like rat urine. Ellie was lying on that mattress. It was a blessing she was unconscious or she'd be whining worse than any Yankee prisoner he'd had the misfortune of dealing with.

One thing for certain, Colum Eduardo Sullivan wasn't sleeping even one night in a boar's nest like this. He found a pile of stained rags on one shelf, grabbed up two and tossed them in the bucket of cold water. He'd seen a cord or two of split wood out behind the shack when he'd gone to the creek. First, a blaze in the fireplace to chase out the chill and then a thorough washing down of the walls, shelves, and floor. Then if Ellie was still alive he intended to work on her hair, find where that the blood was coming from and see just how bad it was. After that, he'd fix food and hopefully she'd be awake enough to get a few bites down.

Miracle of miracles, the chimney wasn't filled with birds' nests or soot and drew very well when he got a fire started. With warmth filling the cabin, snow falling outside, and Ellie still breathing shallowly, he started cleaning. Standing on one of the two chairs he found tossed out the back door, he began with the ceiling, washing away cobwebs, wasp nests and an accumulation of dirt and dust dating back to before the war. He wasn't sure if it was the Civil War or the Revolutionary War or maybe one mentioned in the Bible.

He checked her every few minutes, but she stayed the same. Breathing ever so shallowly with a definite rasp in her chest. Pneumonia most likely. He'd seen the disease many, many times during the war. Most of the time the soldiers didn't last long when they got it.

Six buckets of water later he was ready to clean the floor. Even if the cabin was dreary with its unpainted wood, two doors and only one small window, at least it was clean. He poured three buckets of water on the floor, most of which ran down between the cracks and under the house. He smiled when he heard a kitten protesting the treatment.

The warmth of the fire soon dried the bare wood walls and floor, and Colum brought in another bucket of water. He poured it into an iron pot he'd found shoved in the corner under a table and set it on the andiron in the fireplace to heat. Then he went outside, wading through two inches of snow to bring in his saddle and bedroll.

Flipping out his blankets near the fire to get them warm, he sighed again. The sky was still gray and the snow was coming down in serious business. He'd be here for days and chances of getting back to Texas before spring now were almighty slim. For that alone, he would stake the man, Turley, out on a hill of red ants, cover him with honey and watch the show.

He added a few cups of boiling water to a bucket full of cold water, swished it around with his hand, rolled up his shirt sleeves and got ready for the worst job of all. He unbuttoned Ellie's dress from the neck all the way to the bottom, removed it and her shoes, rolled her stockings down and slipped them from her slender feet, and set his mouth in a tight line when he saw all the bruises on her legs and arms. A hill of red ants was too good for the likes of Turley. The man was a monster.

Colum tried to wash the blood from her hair with a clean cloth but it wasn't working so he leaned her head back over the edge of the cot and poured the water directly on her head. The lye soap he carried in his saddlebags didn't have the rose or lavender scent that ladies liked but at least it cleaned her hair. Carefully readjusting her on the cot, he went back to the creek for more water. It took two buckets full of warm water before he had washed all the soap from her long, blond tresses and found the head wound to be healing. Most likely a doctor would have sutured it, but Turley hadn't been interested in getting Ellie medical attention. There'd be a scar for sure but her pretty blond hair would cover it. He didn't have any idea how to make her hair look like it did in Love's Valley. She did something with it at the nape of her neck but he wasn't a lady's maid.

He dried it as best he could with the cleanest of the rags

he'd found and then braided it in one long rope, much like he did the horses' tails before he put them in a show in north Texas. He used the next bucket of water to wash the grime from her face, hands and legs, knowing the whole time that if she awoke now she'd give him the back side of a tongue lashing. The more he washed, the more the rage built in him. What he'd thought was dirt in some places was in reality deep dark bruises.

When he finished he slipped his arms under her and moved her to the clean bed he'd made next to the warmth of the fire. He wouldn't cover her. Not with the fever raging in her body. The last camp he'd been in before the war ended he'd seen the young doctor argue with the older one about a condition just like this. The older one was of the opinion that the patient should be wrapped in layers of blankets to sweat the fever out of his body. The younger one declared it only made the body hotter and the fever higher. Colum didn't know which one won the argument. He was called away for a tracking job before a conclusion was reached. But he'd often thought of that and he agreed with the younger doctor.

Because of that, he didn't cover Ellie. She moaned and mumbled Monroe's name again but didn't open her eyes. Colum wasn't sure she could open them even if she was lucid and awake. One was swollen worse than the other but the good one looked pretty rugged. He made sure she was comfortable and then picked up the straw tick and carried it out the back door, tossing it behind the wood pile. If the rats wanted it for a winter home then they were welcome to it. At least they could provide a ready supply of food for the cats if they took up abode that close to the house.

Back inside, he stood the two cots on their ends in the corner of the room. He used the rope strung back and forth across the rails to lash them together at right angles. By setting it just right he made a private little alcove for Ellie where she could use the chamber pot in privacy if she lived. They'd have to use the bedroll blankets to drape over the cots, but if she needed to be behind the cots then she wouldn't be lying down anyway. One of the two rickety chairs had a woven cane bottom so he removed that, leaving only the rim of a seat. He set one of the several buckets he'd found under it. He'd seen that done in a makeshift military hospital in Virginia for a patient who couldn't go to the outhouse.

"There, a fancy woman's brand new water closet," he grinned. "Sorry we don't have a fancy little washstand with a porcelain bowl and pitcher, my lady."

"Hello the house," a loud booming voice came from outside, making Colum jump, grab the gun from his holster and spin around, half expecting to see those Yankee varmints storming the house.

"Hello the house," the voice came again.

Hurriedly, Colum yanked his Henry rifle from one side of his saddle and stood it just inside the door frame. The Colt Walker found a home in the small of his back tucked into his belt. He slipped his regular Colt back into the holster but left it untied, and patted the derringer he carried on his leg to make sure it was still in place. Then he opened the front door.

"Who are you?" a tinker asked from the seat of his wagon.

"Who are you?" Colum asked right back.

"Why, I'm Zebediah. Fix anything you need. Sell you anything you don't need. How'd you come to be here? I just passed Turley and his buddies a couple of hours ago over in Shade Valley. Said they'd left a woman in the shack and I could have a bit of sport if she was still alive," he spit a stream of tobacco juice over the side of the wagon.

"They your friends?" Colum asked.

"Wouldn't call them friends. Just know them, that's all. Turley trapped here last winter but swore he wouldn't do it again. So you takin' over the trappin' here?" Zebediah asked.

"Might be," Colum rested his hand on the butt of the Colt on his hip.

"Hey, don't go gettin' trigger happy now, son. I ain't a mind to run you off. Ain't no nevermind to me what you do this winter. Ain't no woman in there anyway, is there? I knowed Turley was lyin' to me even when I give him my finest bottle of snake oil for her," Zebediah talked too much and too fast revealing his nervousness.

"There's a woman in here all right," Colum said. "Reckon you can have your bit of sport if you'd like. You ever had the small pox?"

"Great God Almighty," Zebediah turned as pale as the snow floating around him. "That low down skunk. I'll poison the next bottle of snake oil I give him."

"I'd buy some supplies you got a notion to sell any," Colum said. "Got anything for the high hot fever that comes just before the pox breaks out? And how about a coffee pot and some coffee. Anything else you got, I'd buy it."

"Got real money? You sound like one of them Confederates. That what you are, son? One of them rebels on his way back home? I ain't taken none of that worthless Confederate paper money," Zebediah said.

"That's exactly what I am, but I got good money to buy with long as you don't try to cheat me." Colum said. "Reckon you could just unload whatever you think I might use this winter and leave it on the ground. I'll lay the money for it about halfway between me and you and that way you won't have to come in the house."

"Ain't you afraid of the pox?" Zebediah hopped off the wagon seat, opened the back door and began to unload. How much could he swindle the stupid rebel out of? He'd asked for something to cure the pox so he'd sell him enough snake oil to kill or cure the woman.

"Naw," Colum shook his head. "Can't get them twice can you?" He hadn't actually lied up to that point. He'd merely asked the man if he had had the pox or if he could get them twice, but he would lie if it meant keeping that burly tinker out of the cabin.

"Is the woman a looker?" Zebediah unloaded a whole case of the magic elixir guaranteed to cure everything from ingrown toenails to dysentery.

"Mighta been at one time. Ain't much to look at right now though," Colum figured he was getting taken for a ride financially but it was better to be overstocked than under in a snowstorm in the mountains.

"Ain't much to look at right now," Ellie repeated hoarsely without opening her eyes. Every fiber in her body ached but in her half-conscious state, she figured she'd died and was floating around somewhere between heaven and earth. That wasn't Monroe's voice talking at the doorway. He had a deeper, more resonant tone. It sounded like a rebel, but it couldn't be. The war had been over for more than a year.

She opened her good eye and the first thing she saw was the blazing flames in the fireplace. Holy smoke, she'd bypassed heaven and gone to hell in her undergarments. Well, she'd told Oscar she'd rather go to hell than spend a night with him. At least it wasn't as hot as she'd always been told it would be. Other than a severely parched throat and the fact that her skin was too warm, it wasn't so bad. She tried desperately to keep her eye open but it snapped shut and the darkness came again.

"Where you headed from here?" Colum asked, watching the man unload two bushels of potatoes and one of carrots.

"Mount Union," Zebediah said. "Got these vegetables from a woman up in the other end of Shade Valley. She wanted several of her pots fixed and a new washbowl and pitcher. Didn't have no money so I took it out in trade. Do that often then sell whatever I trade for. Works most of the time."

"Where's Mount Union?" Colum asked.

"Well now, it would be back up the road a little piece, then turn back to the right and wind down the mountain 'bout six miles. Me and old Boss there can make it since we know the way and she could take me down the road blindfolded. Smart old horse even if she is gettin' up in years," Zebediah took out a stack of blankets. "You going to need these?" he asked nervously. The man up there in the doorway could still shoot him dead. After all, he was a rebel on the run with a gun.

"I'll take them. You got a feather pillow in there?" Colum asked.

"Got two and a set of them fancy pillow cases with embroidery on the edges, too. Woman wanted a bottle of elixir," Zebediah explained.

Colum nodded. "How far is Mount Union from Shirleysburg?"

"About seven miles. You can go up Blacklog Valley into Orbisonia. That'd be a sight farther and then four more back into Shirleysburg, or you can go down the mountain like I said and get into Mount Union which is where I plan on wintering. Got me a little cabin up on the range near Allenport, couple of miles this side of Mount Union. By the time spring comes I'll have cabin fever and be ready for me and Boss to hit the road again," he said. "Now that's about all I'm carryin' with me you'd be interested in havin'. That'd come to about twenty dollars, I'd reckon."

Colum was faintly surprised. He figured the man would goad him much worse than twenty dollars. "Seems fair since you brought it right to me," he said. "I'd give you twenty-five if you'd carry a letter for me and post it wherever you could. Needs to go to Shirleysburg."

"Five dollars just to post a letter?" Zebediah cocked his head to one side.

"That's what I said," Colum nodded.

"Be glad to," Zebediah said. "You just put it right there on that stump with the money and I'll take it with me."

"I won't be but a minute," Colum said, edging back into the shack and rifling through his saddlebags for writing equipment. All good soldiers carried what they needed to send a letter home and he'd never gotten past the habit.

Home soon as we can travel.

CES

"Thank you," he said as he laid the letter addressed to Douglass Hamilton on the stump along with the money for the supplies.

"I'd a mailed it for nothing," Zebediah grabbed both and trotted back to the wagon. "But I ain't refusin' no money. Reckon you know I charged you high for some of that stuff. It was to make up for not havin' that woman in there. Some days you just got to pay."

A smile broke across Colum's face. Zebediah could take his wounded pride and disappointment on across the mountain with him and nurse both all winter. Colum would have paid twenty dollars in good money just for the information that there was a town that close. When Ellie was well enough they'd walk down the mountain, catch a stage over to Shirleysburg and hire a buggy to get them back into Love's Valley.

"Wouldn't want to sell old Boss there would you?" Colum asked.

"Sell Boss?" Zebediah roared. "Wouldn't sell this horse to you even if you offered me a hundred dollars in pure gold."

"Can't blame a man for tryin'," Colum took his stand in the doorway and waited until Zebediah and his wagon were completely out of sight before he began carrying all the supplies into the shack.

Ellie reached up to touch the hurt place on her head and realized even in the foggy state she was in that her hair was clean and hung in a ropy braid over her shoulder. She didn't feel quite as hot with the fever as she did when Turley left.

She moved her feet, happy to realize the shackles were gone. She hurt too bad to be dead like she thought when she regained consciousness the last time. Was that today or yesterday?

Very carefully, she opened her eyes. Good grief, what was Turley doing sitting at the table peeling potatoes? He'd only brought her cold bread and a few pieces of jerky the whole last week. The normal stench of the place had disappeared and been replaced by the smell of good clean lye soap.

She narrowed her eyes, the one swollen the worst shutting completely. It wasn't Turley or that friend of his, Alvie. The hair was darker. He was shorter and a quite a bit more muscular. Not nearly as fat around the middle or as dirty. But then he was sitting down with his back to her and she was lying flat on the floor . . . in her drawers and camisole. Her tattered dress, the very one she'd worn out to muck out horse stables that fatal morning, was no where in sight. She pulled the blanket around her body, rolling up in it like a mummy.

She watched him for several moments and then realized he was humming. Merciful Mary, Mother of Jesus, what had happened since she screamed at the rat? The place was clean. Some fellow was making food. A nice blaze burned happily in the fireplace, and she was clean.

Cold air from under the house drifted up through the cracks in the floor to chill her bare feet. She drew them up inside the confines of the blanket and listened to the wind whistle down the valley. Was it morning or night? She turned her head slowly to look out the window but everything was white. Snow. She'd thought she smelled the first snow of the season when Turley left the door open.

"Who are you and what are you doing?" she whispered.

Colum looked over his shoulder. "Since you're awake, it's time to begin your medicine. The quicker you either get well or die the faster I can go home to Texas. At least you've woke up in your right mind. I wondered if you might be affected."

"You!" Ellie could scarcely believe her eyes. There stood the second worst man in the whole world. Douglass's brother, Colum Sullivan. A rebel. A confederate. A worthless piece of manhood who still bore the mark on his cheek where she'd scratched him the first time she met him. She'd almost rather have been holed up in a blizzard with Turley.

"Yep, me," Colum picked up a pan of potatoes and carrots and carried them to the pot hanging in the fireplace. "We'll have soup for supper. I've got some jerky to shave in it for a little flavor."

"I won't eat anything you fix," Ellie declared feverishly, wishing the darkness would claim her again.

"Oh, yes you will, Ellie," Colum kneeled in front of her. "You don't have to like me but you'll have to endure me until you get well enough for us to walk out of this place and get you home. Until then you'll eat and take your medicine. I don't want to be holed up with the likes of you any more than you want to be with me. But I done promised my sister I'd bring you back to Love's Valley, and I'll do it."

His light brown eyes met her clear blue ones, anger sizzling when two gazes collided in the six inches of space separating their noses. He really was quite handsome with jet black hair, square chin and pecan-colored eyes with darker flecks. It didn't matter, though, because he was a rebel. One of those miserable men who burned her home in Chambersburg, leaving her parents dead.

Colum stirred the soup pot for a moment then went back to his work station, keeping his back turned to the woman. Elspeth Hamilton, Ellie for short, wasn't an ugly woman by any means. Not even with the fever making her fair skin a deep pink. Blue eyed, as tall as Colum, and built right nice, but Colum wasn't interested in anything but getting the shrew home so he could go to his own home in north Texas.

She'd attacked him the first day he'd arrived to rescue his sister and there'd been no love lost between them in the following week. He still bore a faint red scab where her fingernails dug into his face.

"What kind of medicine?" she asked.

"I have no idea. A man named Zebediah stopped and I bought whatever he had," Colum said without blinking.

"Snake oil," she moaned. "Lord, I hate that elixir. He sells it to Aunt Laura once a year. She uses it for everything."

"Well, you're going to take it. I figure you've either got or are about to get pneumonia," Colum didn't back up an inch.

"Can I have a drink of water afterwards?" she asked.

"I don't care if you drink a whole bucket full," he answered.

"Then go get it. Don't just sit there staring at me like I was some kind of circus attraction," she snapped.

"Fever didn't fry out your smart mouth," he mumbled as he went for the medicine and one of the two spoons he found on a shelf.

"I'm only hateful to you," she said.

"Oh, were you sweet to the man who had you shackled to the wall?" he smarted right back as he knelt before her and poured up a spoonful of the vile smelling liquid. It had to be half or more pure grain alcohol since it hadn't frozen in the bottle. Even that would have healing properties, though. And goodness only knew, if he gave her enough of it, she might get drunk and sweeten up a little. *Not with your luck*, his conscience said tartly. *She'd make a mean drunk.*

"I intend to kill that man some day," she said opening her mouth and preparing herself for the bitter taste.

"Stand in line," Colum said.

"Lord, that tastes like pure evil," she said. "It tastes as bad as I hate rebels."

"Good! With that much hate, you'll live," he said. "Now lay back down and I'll have supper ready in a little while."

"Don't you tell me what to do," she said. "I'm tired of lay-ing down. I want to sit."

"Suit yourself," he said and disappeared out the back door, leaving her to do whatever she wanted while he set a live trap next to the river. They'd need meat and if he set up another kind of trap he'd no doubt find a momma cat in it come morning. Then there'd be all those whining kittens. Ellie would want to bring them in the house and take care of them. No, he'd just set a live trap and hope for a nice big fat raccoon or a rabbit. Neither one was as tasty as beef from a north Texas ranch but they'd keep body and soul together until he could get back there.

"I hate you," Ellie whispered. "I'll drink bottles of that vile stuff to get well so I can go home and be rid of you."

Chapter Three

Ellie awoke to the good aroma of the stew. She and Colum had barely said two words the day before. She nodded when he asked her if she was hungry and didn't bother to thank him for taking care of her. Why should she? No doubt, Monroe was paying him handsomely for his work. Besides if Monroe wasn't, then Ellie would. She had money and she'd be damned if she'd be beholden to a sorry rebel for saving her life.

"I'm having a bath," she declared.

"If you haven't got pneumonia, then you'll get it, bathing in a drafty old place like this," Colum said.

"Death would be better than smelling like I do," she said.

"Don't you dare die on me," Colum narrowed his light-brown eyes and scowled at her. "I've got a saddle to carry out of this god-forsaken place. I can't carry it and you both. If you die because you think you stink then I swear I'll bury you right out there beside this place."

"You would, you dirty rebel," Ellie shot right back at him. "You'd carry a saddle before you would me?"

"Yes, ma'am, I would," Colum dipped up the stew and handed her a bowl full with one hand and a spoon with the other.

"Show's what kind of man you are," she retorted.

"Yes, ma'am, it probably does. Saddle's been good to me. You haven't. That saddle and I've been through a lot together. It hasn't ever scratched blood from my cheek. It doesn't pout or want a bath in the middle of a snowstorm," he said.

"I'm having a bath and I don't pout," she said, amazed that the soup tasted so good. They'd eaten the same thing for breakfast, dinner and supper the day before. Potatoes, carrots, onions and rabbit boiled together with a little salt and pepper thrown in to bring out the flavor. Things could be worse. They had been worse before Colum arrived. She only had bread and precious little water. Compared to those days, she was wallowing in the lap of luxury.

"I suppose you'll want my extra suit of clothes to wear while your things dry?" A grin played at the corners of his mouth.

Ellie hadn't thought that far. A bath wouldn't do her a bit of good if she had to put the undergarments back on her body without washing them. To parade around in front of him wrapped in a blanket was one thing. To do so with no unmentionables under the blanket was another. That would strip of her of her dignity as well as her reputation.

Her integrity already lay in shreds. No one would believe those abominable men hadn't taken advantage of her before they left her for dead. They'd believe she was kidnapped. They'd never doubt that she'd been beaten. But men of that caliber didn't just walk away and not have their way with a defenseless woman. Not unless they considered her an ugly old maid not even worthy of their contemptible affections. Either was enough to keep any decent man out of Love's Valley and away from courting Ellie. Tongues would make that sympathetic, condemning noise behind fans at socials when the story was told. Ellie set her jaw in defense just thinking about it. They'd forgive her since she had no control over it, but they'd pity her for the ordeal she'd been through.

God, save me from their self-righteous pity, she thought,

28 *Carolyn Brown*

unclenching her jaw and cramming in another spoon of soup. Soup, which had suddenly lost all flavor.

However, when the whole community surrounding Love's Valley found that she'd actually spent days and days holed up in a cabin with a man with no chaperone, they'd shun her for sure. When they found out the man was a ex-Confederate, she'd be lucky if they didn't pay Turley and Alvie to come back and finish the job they'd begun. She bit back a sob. One whimper and she'd be hysterical for sure and no one could fault her a split second for it, either. She'd been through more than most women could endure this past week. Watching her favorite cousin Monroe fall in love with Douglass Sullivan, a half-Irish, half-Mexican, and a rebel thrown in to boot. Barely coming to grips with that idea when she broke off her engagement. Then the very next morning, finding herself kidnapped and chained to the wall in a dirty trapper's cabin. And now to have to dress herself in men's clothing just to wash the grime from her body. It was too much. But Colum Sullivan wouldn't see her cry, not if she had to bring blood to the inside of her lip. Besides if she let one little whimper escape, one tiny tear fall from her eyes or one slight quiver in her chin, she'd bawl for a week. This wasn't the time for wallowing in self pity. Later when she was back home, she might lock herself in her room and give in to a crying jag. She inhaled deeply and promised herself a good old-fashioned womanly weeping fit when she got home.

"Yes, I would like to wear your extra suit of clothing until mine is dry," she said, voice as void of emotion as she could make it.

"I'll lay them inside your water closet," he said, just as cool. "I'll have to heat some water but it should be done by the time you finish eating, slow as you are."

She didn't answer. Swallowing around the lump in her throat took every bit of self control she could muster. Speaking without flushing the knot out in the form of a river of tears was an impossibility. She kept telling herself over and over that she was a strong woman and Colum wasn't stealing her self-respect by seeing her shed tears.

Setting her empty bowl aside after she'd finished eating, Ellie made her weak legs carry her across the room to the makeshift water closet. She dropped the blanket she'd shrouded herself in since she'd awakened in nothing but her underwear, stepped out of her drawers and camisole and methodically began to bathe. Using the lye soap and a clean cloth Colum had found somewhere, she washed her face, long slender neck and shoulders. Where had he found that clean washcloth? She wondered. It certainly hadn't been there the whole week she'd been kept captive. Nothing was clean in the cabin then. Dreary as it was now, at least it was clean and smelled nice. She'd have to give that much to Colum Sullivan. He knew how to keep house. She continued washing her body, shivering and hurrying a bit when the cold wind whistled through the dead trees outside and crept through the cracks in the floorboards to chill her damp skin.

"You needin' another bucket of water warmed for your hair?" he called from the other side of the makeshift walls.

"No, I'm not washing my hair. It's still squeaky clean from the washing you gave it," she said, her voice quivering with the cold.

Colum grinned. So she was a bit cold, was she? Well, it served her right, wanting a bath when she had just snuggled up so close to death. He'd have to give her a little credit even if it galled him to do so. Not many woman could have survived what she'd suffered. Douglass told him that Ellie hated rebels because her folks had been killed in the fire in the battle of Chambersburg. That alone would have sent a southern belle into vapors for the rest of her life, but not Elspeth Hamilton. She still had enough strength left to jump on his back and scratch blood from his cheek when all he was trying to do was rescue his sister from that low down Yankee who possibly had kidnapped her. As it turned out, the Yankee hadn't kidnapped Douglass at all. Truth be told, it was almost the reverse. His ornery sister had covered her own misdeeds with a few lies to put more time between the time she ran away from home and the time her brothers would rescue her.

No woman in the world had more determination and fire than Douglass Esmerelda Sullivan, now Hamilton. Born into an Irish-Mexican family following six boys, she'd grown up pampered, spoiled, and yet meaner than a constipated rattlesnake. Leaning back in the chair, resting his feet on the edge of the table, memories racing through his mind of his sister, he had to admit, Douglass Esmerelda was a strong woman, but not an ounce stronger than Elspeth Hamilton. No, sir. Not one sliver of an ounce.

Ellie slipped her legs into the soft, worn trousers. They weren't so very different from her drawers. Both covered her from waist to ankle. What was the big deal about women wearing them on the outside when they wore essentially the same thing beneath their clothing. Only the trousers weren't made from white lawn, nor did they have lace around the edges topped with delicate embroidered roses. The vision of stubborn, aloof Colum Sullivan wearing a pair of trousers with lace and roses on them brought a weak chuckle that erupted into a full-fledged giggle.

"And what is so funny?" Colum asked, pushing his legs away from the table and letting the chair fall with a loud clump to the floor. Women! He'd never understand them. Ever since he rescued her from the shackles she'd treated him like a hired servant that she despised. Not one smile. Not a thank you. Just a nose held up so high if it rained she'd drown for sure. No conversation. All she did was sleep, eat and stare at the fire as if she were in a trance. And now she laughed!

"Oh, no," he mumbled, rolling his eyes upward. She'd finally gone stark raving mad. He'd given her credit for strength too soon. She'd taken one look at her body covered with brushes, realized the way people would pity her and had lost it all in a moment. Now he'd have to deal with a crazy woman instead of an uppity one.

Giggles turned into hiccups as she finished buttoning his shirt and stepped out into the room where he sat with his head buried in his hands. "What's the matter with you? Never heard a woman laugh before?" she asked, the chill in her voice even colder than the drafts off the foot of snow creeping up through the floorboards.

Colum jerked his head up. Her eyes weren't filled with madness, but rather were glittering with amusement. And oh my, he had never seen a woman look so fine in men's clothing. Legs as long as his, well-rounded bottom, trousers pulled in with a white drawstring around a wispy thin waist, shirt tucked in but leaving little doubt that she was well-endowed in the bosom area. If he'd had to recite a Hail Mary or pass on into eternity, he'd have had to ask for final rites because he couldn't utter a word.

"Well, haven't you?" she asked again.

"Of course," he managed hoarsely. "What were you laughing at anyway?"

"The idea of sewing some lace on the bottom of these trousers and maybe embroidering some flowers on the sides. Don't you think they'd be right fetching with roses entwined from the ankles up to the hips?" She turned and cocked a hip out toward him.

"You wouldn't dare!" He narrowed brown eyes, his forehead furrowing in wrinkles of disgust.

"I might if we have to stay in this place much longer. The boredom is enough to drive a man to drink and a woman to embroidering roses on men's trousers," she declared flippantly. "But right now the bath has worn me plumb out. I'll have to wash my things after a while. Guess there's no hurry, is there? We can't leave this place until the snow stops."

"Melts," he said. "Until the snow melts."

"Stops," she said. "When it stops and the sun comes out

we'll walk down the mountain side but let me tell you one thing, Mr. Sullivan. You'll be carrying that saddle the whole way if you love it so much. I'm not shouldering it even a tenth of a mile." She stretched out on her pallet in front of the fire, tucking her feet and securing in the folds of the blanket. The floor was hard but Colum had folded two other blankets in half, creating four layers between her and the drafts. *Warm*, she thought. *Toasty warm just when I thought I was going to be bear bait.*

"You can't walk six miles in the snow with pneumonia," he argued.

"I don't have pneumonia. The fever is gone. I'm weak and I've still got a cough but it's not pneumonia. My chest doesn't ache. It doesn't feel like it's got a brick laying down inside it. And it doesn't burn. I know what pneumonia is. I nursed more than one soldier through it during the war." Heat waves radiated from the glowing embers and penetrated through the blanket into her skin. Soothing. Wonderful. She would never take such a luxury for granted again.

"You did what?" he asked, his curiosity piqued. She'd just said more in three minutes than she'd said in two days.

"I helped at the hospital in Chambersburg during the war," she said. "Believe me, I know the signs of pneumonia. And we will get out of here soon as we can, Colum Sullivan. My strength will build and so will the snowdrifts. Not only do I know the signs of pneumonia but I've lived in this area for the past two years. Once the snow starts, winter is here. Some will melt when the sun comes out but it'll just keep piling up. All of it won't melt until March, and I'm not living here with you until then. Now, I'm going to sleep. Rest builds strength."

"Well, sleep a long time," he said sarcastically, thinking of all the supplies he'd shelled out good money to purchase and would have to be left in the cabin. "I might need some help getting this saddle down the mountain and a good strong woman would be handy."

"In your dreams, Rebel," she mumbled as she shut her eyes. The last thing she thought before she fell asleep was how in the world could she be so comfortable in a cabin with someone of Colum Sullivan's caliber?

Chapter Four

"What are you doing to the blanket?" Ellie asked, watching Colum lay one out long ways on the floor and fold it in half, straightening all the corners so it lay perfectly. It seemed like a waste of time to her. After they'd gone tomorrow morning, whoever came into the cabin looking for a place to rest or to take up the trapping business wouldn't care if the blankets were folded so proper. They'd be looking for a warm fire and maybe a leftover can of beans.

"We are leaving out of here tomorrow morning at first light, no?" he asked, not taking his eyes from the job at hand.

"Yes, we are," she said.

"And what do you intend to wear on this day long journey down the mountain? The tinker said it was six miles from the turn, but it's half a day's walk to that turn. Do you think the sun, if it decides to grace us by appearing, is going to keep you warm enough in nothing but your undergarments? Your dress is in tatters and useless. Thank goodness you were wearing work boots when they kidnapped you," he said, finally getting the blanket just like he wanted.

Ellie had figured she'd wear his extra pants and shirt and maybe use a blanket for a shawl. When the idea of piercing,

wet cold entered her mind, she'd pushed it aside. Back in the far reaches of her brain where bad memories were banished.

"I'm a strong woman. I can make it in pants and shirt if you can," she said.

"Well, I can't," he said simply. "I'm not going to freeze and neither are you when I can put together a Leine-and-Brat and top it off with a poncho."

"What's that?" she asked.

"Come and lay on this blanket," he said. "Put your shoulders at the top and stretch your arms straight out."

"Are you teasing me, Mr. Sullivan?" she asked.

"Not for a minute. When we have your Brat made, then I'll need your assistance in making mine. A Brat is an Irish garment. My Dad taught me about them when I was a small child. In Ireland, it's made with the clan's own special plaid wool, but since I don't have any of the Sullivan plaid, this blanket will fill the bill." *And besides, I wouldn't be clothing you in the Sullivan plaid for that would mean I have asked for your hand in marriage,* he thought.

While she carefully laid on the folded blanket, he kept talking. "In the war, I was sent to northern Virginia. In the mountains there with the militia. Us Texas boys weren't used to the snow or the cold, especially lasting so long. We lost more soldiers because of the effects of the cold than we did to the Yank's guns. I taught them to make Leine-and-Brat, and even ponchos from blankets when we could get them. At least some of us survived."

"And the Leine? What is that?" she asked, suddenly interested in the way he used his hunting knife to cut a hole in the blanket evidently for her to put her head through.

"The Leine is a robe type thing or long shirt if you want to think about it like that. Something like you'd think of a monk wearing. I'll use the part I cut from the bottom to put sleeves into the openings there," he said, drawing a heavy thread through the eye of a needle.

"You carry a needle and thread?" she asked, almost angry

at him for not telling her he had access to them. She could have been entertaining herself the past four days by stitching something.

"Since that first winter in Virginia, I'm never without my guns or my sewing equipment. Both have saved my life," he said, carefully cutting the bottom edge of the blanket away and forming the wool into two tubes that would suffice as sleeves. The sewing didn't need to hold up all winter like it did in Virginia. It did have to stay together long enough to get her from the cabin to Love's Valley.

"So the Leine is a monk's garment. What's the Brat thing?"

"Not *lain,*" he said. "It's pronounced *lay-nuh* and the Brat is said like there is a *w* between the *a* and *t*. Think Irish tones even if they do offend your English ears."

"I am English. At least my mother was but the Irish brogue doesn't offend my ears nearly so much as the Rebels do my eyes," she smarted off.

"Oh, and I have given my Irish word as well as my Mexican one that I will bring you home safely. What a pity," he fired right back without missing a stitch.

"Hmpph," she snorted. "You still haven't answered my question."

"A Brat is the other garment, a long piece of wool, wrapped around the shoulders and tied with a belt, on the outside mind you. It's like the coat or jacket. That's what made the Irish different. They belted their tartan on the outside. It will be the piece that drapes around all that pretty blond hair and keeps the biting cold wind from your ears and neck. The Leine will keep your arms and body warm, the Brat will be yet another layer over the top of it. Then I shall use the last two blankets for the third layer which will be a Mexican poncho. Ever seen one of those?" he asked.

"Only in pictures, and don't you be so hateful. Monroe won't pay you if I tell him you treated me like a child," she sniffed.

"Pay me?" He stopped his work and stared deeply into her blue eyes. "Pay me?" He said again incredulously. "I'm not paid help, Miss Elspeth Hamilton. I'm family and family doesn't take pay. Leave it to a Yankee to have that kind of thinking in her head. No wonder there was a war. You unemotional Yankees never could understand the passionate feelings we southerners have. Add that to the passion of Mexicans and Irish and you really wouldn't have a clue about my way of life."

"You mean you came out here just to find me because Douglass is part of the family now?" she asked skeptically.

"She has taken a great liking to you," Colum went back to his sewing, refusing to look at her eyes again. A man could suffocate in those blue eyes. Faith and begora, but he could die a happy man with his fingers tangled up in all that blond hair and his face so close to those eyes he could feel the fire from them on his face.

"Hmm," Ellie mumbled, turning her face back to the fire. She didn't need to watch him make some kind of medieval garments. Evidently he could fashion them quite well without her input, and the very thought that he was there because he wanted to be and not because of money was already lying heavy on her heart. So he'd come because Douglass had asked him, most likely had to beg him on her knees since he hated Ellie so badly. Just because she scratched his pretty face and left a faint scar right there above the dimple. It sure didn't mar his handsome looks one whit. Of course, with all his southern gentleman vanity, it could keep him from ever being the most gorgeous man to ever step into a general store. But she doubted it. Even with the scar, he'd still out-rank any man she'd ever seen, even her favorite cousin, Monroe, who now held second place in the good looks department.

Neither of them slept well that night. Both greeted the first rays of morning slipping through the pale gray skies with heightened senses. A long walk lay ahead of them with no place to stop between the cabin and Allenport and the sun hid its face behind a solid wall of gray clouds. Once they stepped out that front door, they'd have to keep going until they reached their destination no matter how tired they were. Even Colum's Leine-and-Brat wouldn't protect them if weariness felled them along the way. They'd freeze in a matter of hours.

Colum busied himself in the dawning hour with two rabbits he'd caught the day before in his traps. He'd skinned them the night before and hung them in the woodshed out back. The cats hadn't been lucky enough to smell them out so that morning he spit roasted them while Ellie combed her hair with her fingertips and rebraided it. Long, luxurious blond hair that mesmerized Colum when she worked with it. But that morning, he didn't have time to dally around watching the strands move between Ellie's fingers, even if it was downright tempting.

"Put on my extra suit of clothing over your underthings," he said. "Then I will help get you dressed."

"I've been dressing myself for years," she retorted but she grabbed the trousers and shirt folded neatly on the table. "Aren't we going to eat the last of those potatoes and carrots?"

"Yes, ma'am. That's breakfast and we'll eat as much as we can force down. The cold will use it up fast and all we've got to take with us is a couple of rabbits to gnaw on while we travel," he said.

"I pitched a couple of potatoes in the fire last night. They should be done by now. Drag them out and we'll wrap them in a cloth. That'll keep our fingers warm a little while and then we can eat them when the warmth is gone," she said.

Colum smiled. So the woman had some common sense after all. Why hadn't he thought of warm potatoes to carry along? Because he was too busy stitching a Leine-and-Brat for each of them, he reminded himself. Hopefully they'd either reach a livery stable in Allenport or make it all the way to the stage station in Mount Union before dark. He didn't want to think about the consequences. Had he been traveling alone, he had no doubt he'd get there, but with a woman, and one who was still a bit weak from ailing, he did have doubts. Serious ones.

Following breakfast, true to his word, Colum dressed her. First the Leine, then the Brat, draping the long length of woolen blanket so it formed a type of hood around her head, belting it on with a three-corded braided rope he'd worked up from the edges he'd cut away from the blankets. "Inside this pouch," he explained as he tied a drawstring reticule onto the braided belt, "is a two-shot derringer. I usually carry it on my leg in a small holster built especially for it. There's too much material between your leg and the gun for it to do you a bit of good, so I'm tying it right here in front. Should you need it, you can get to it by pulling this string. That will open the top. This poncho I'm about to throw over you will hide your hands. Just remember you've only got two shots. Make them count."

"I can shoot," she said, too warm beneath the layers of wool blankets.

"Good," he said. "Go on out on the stoop and wait. If you stay in here any longer you'll build a layer of sweat and it will freeze when you are outside."

She did what he said without an argument, thinking that the cold might feel better than the extra warmth. The first step out the door brought a gasp. Wind swept through the valley in a rush and bit into the tender skin on her face. She'd never endure a whole day of fighting against such a force.

"Ready?" he said, opening the door and joining her, his saddle on one shoulder, both hands holding it firmly there.

"The wind is fierce," she said.

"Pick up the corner of your Brat like this and pull it across your nose. That will keep it and your lips from frost bite. That's good, right up to your eyes," he said, letting go of the saddle with his right hand long enough to do the same and demonstrate. "Now, let's go."

And they went.

The potato worked for maybe fifteen minutes then the warmth was gone completely. She wondered what he'd done with his since it took both his hands to keep the saddle steady on his shoulder. At least he had gloves, but she couldn't find a covetous bone in her body as she trudged along beside him. She didn't have to carry a saddle so she could wrap her fingers in any one of the layers of wool wrappings. She'd have to remember the idea of all these things. Especially the poncho. It would be wonderful to use for dashing out to the barn in the early morning hours to milk the cows or check the horses.

"So how is it you know so much about the Irish and the Mexicans?" she broke the silence two hours later. Even beneath the wool her warm breath was having a difficult time keeping her nose and cheeks from freezing. The rest of her body wasn't stone cold yet but it wasn't toasty either. The many layers trapped her body heat, but even that had a tough battle with the never ending cold wind.

"Daddy is Irish like I told you. He raised me on Irish folklore. Rest assured, the snow fairies won't be interested in you since you are wearing a Leine. Even if it is a man's Leine," he said.

"You've wrapped me up in men's clothing. Irish male robes?" she said, aghast. "The snow fairies might be able to see beneath them and know that I'm not an Irish man and get me after all."

"Well, well, my lady, you do have a sense of humor hiding down there in all that stiff English blood," he managed a chuckle. The saddle got heavier with every mile, but he couldn't let his mind dwell on that now. Not when they had so far to go, and not when it carried the food for the day and ammunition to keep them out of trouble. His Henry rifle and Colt pistol, both loaded, rested in the special sheaths on the side of the saddle. The belt and holster for the other Colt provided the belt for his own Leine. He prayed he'd reach Love's Valley without firing any of them.

"I'm considered quite the witty one in my circles," she said stoically. Sweet baby Jesus, she'd walked forever it seemed. And if she didn't stop thinking blasphemous words, her father was going to rise up out of his grave and give her that mean look he'd used to control her when she was a child. The sun hid behind a solid curtain of gray that threatened to spill more snow on them at any moment. Without the sun, she couldn't tell how far they'd walked or what time it was. She did know that the morning stew was gone now because her stomach had begun to grumble for more food. She'd slipped the potato beneath the folds in the Brat and seriously considered dragging it out and chewing on it as she walked.

"In your circles there is no wit," he said.

She gave him a glare meant to fry him beneath all those silly blankets. "In your circles there is no tact."

"Hey, honey, I'm half-Irish. That means I speak my mind freely and give my love just as freely. But only to the one who has held my heart in her soul from the beginning. When I find her I'll know she's the one the gods have kept special for me. The Irish are a happy lot. My father is true to his Sullivan blood and raised us to be the same. The other half is passionate Mexican which gives me the right to argue and fight even more than the Irish. The Mexicans are just as happy as the Irish so I'm double blessed. As much as if I'd truly been raised in either country by either set of ancestors. But you are right, tact is not my long suit. I speak my mind and you can live with it until we get you safely home. After that I'll see to it I stay out of the way of that sharp tongue you were blessed with."

"That is the best news I've had since I found out we won the war," she told him bluntly.

"And if my baby sister, Douglass, had been allowed to join, the tides might have been different," he threw back at her.

Carolyn Brown

"If I'd been allowed to fight, it would have been over in a year," she tossed right back.

"Ah, a woman after my own heart," he chuckled.

The laughter made her even more angry. "Don't you laugh at me. You men are so bull-headed, you just had to have a war, didn't you? Just had to tear the country apart, burning and looting, and destroying families. If you'd left it to us women, we would have sat down over a cup of hot tea and discussed it for a week. We'd have come up with a workable solution and there would have been no bloodshed."

"Sure you would have darlin'," he chuckled again. Her quick wit made him wonder if perhaps her mother had actually sprung from the Irish and not the cold English at all. *Now why did I have to think the word cold?* He berated himself, feeling the chill leeching through the layers and to his flesh. Before long it would penetrate his bones and make his feet numb. He'd been in that place many times during the war, but it sure didn't make him look forward to going there again. As a matter of fact, he'd promised himself if he ever got warm again after that Virginia winter, he'd never leave Texas again. A broken promise that weighed on his heart right then.

"I'll tell you about the Irish fairies while we walk to make the time pass quickly," he said, ignoring the wicked looks she shot at him. So she thought she could win the war, did she? She was so almighty important that she could have brought two fiercely loyal factions to their knees and brought about a compromise with a cup of tea. If that was the case, he'd sure like to know where to purchase a whole shipload of her kind of tea. That's just the thing that made her act like she was really some kind of English royalty, now wasn't it?

"And what if I don't want to hear anything stupid like a lesson on fairies?" she asked.

"Then don't listen," he said. "I've a mind to refresh my own memory about the fairies and I'll tell it aloud to myself. You can shut your mean old English ears if you've a mind to do that. Otherwise, just walk beside me and listen if you want."

"I'm not mean, Mr. Sullivan," she said.

"That would be Colum, ma'am. My Daddy isn't even Mr. Sullivan. Mr. Sullivan was my grandfather. And mean, like beauty, is in the eye of the beholder," Colum said.

"So you think I'm beautiful and mean?" she asked.

"You are always and forever beautiful. As lovely as the fairies, but as mean as a rattlesnake most of the time," he said.

She smiled beneath the covering on her face. So he thought she was always and forever beautiful. Not an ugly old maid, like Turley had called her, but as gorgeous as his lovely fairies. "Well, are you going to tell me about the fairies or not?" she said shortly.

He sighed and suppressed another chuckle. He might not have actually kissed the Blarney Stone himself, but his father, Michael, swore he'd put his lips upon it once upon a time when he was a young boy. And Colum was his son, after all, and if he had to keep company with Ellie, then he just might charm some of that mean out of her broken heart and spirit.

"Well, if you're insisting on a lesson in the Irish fairies, then I could be persuaded to oblige you. Perhaps if the telling robs me of my strength, you'd oblige me then in carrying my saddle part of the way down the mountain?" he asked.

"I will not," she exclaimed, only to bring on a deep, resonant chuckle that let her know he'd been teasing her. Did all Irish men have such a sense of humor? She wondered. Sweet baby Jesus, and she'd think whatever she liked, she said silently to her father's haunting eyes for using the savior's name in vain.

"Just kidding, *querida, a ghra,*" he said. "That means sweetheart, darlin', one in Spanish and one in Irish," he explained. He didn't give her the absolute true meaning of *a ghra*, which was *O love!* She would have kicked him all the way to Love's Valley had he told her that. Besides, teasing her about being a sweetheart or a darling was one thing. Using the word love in the same sentence with her name was sure to bring him bad luck. He could never love a woman like Elspeth Hamilton. She was English. She was a Yankee. She was mean. She was bullheaded. Just to name a few of the traits he'd never accept in a woman he would allow to lay claim upon his heart.

"I'm not your sweetheart, darlin', honey or anything else, Colum Sullivan," she snapped. "Just get on with your tale and entertain me."

"Ah, I can't," he said, raising both eyebrows. "Before a man can break into the tales of the fairies, he must have something in his heart for the woman he's telling. A true Irishman would never have to tell an Irish lass about the fairies. She would already know, so it would be an outsider who'd be hearing the tale and she would have to hold a special place to appreciate the effort of the special story."

"One minute ago you were bound and determined to refresh your memory by telling yourself the story and I could just listen if I wanted to or I could close my ears. Now it's got to be that I'm your sweetheart?" she reminded him, suddenly enjoying the banter.

"'Tis the way of it," he said. "Pretend," he whispered loudly. "Should there be a banshee around these parts she might be listening. The banshees come across the water, for sure, you know, to check on the transported Irish. So pretend that you are my sweetheart so she won't be casting a spell on me."

"You are a rogue," Ellie said. "But okay, for the length of the tale, I'll be your sweetheart. Now what is it about the fairies?"

"Well now, first a little lesson, then I'll tell you a fair story of an Irish lass who spoke to the fairies. In Ireland two fairy types exist, the trooping fairies and the solitary fairies. The trooping fairies can be found in merry bans about the hawthorn tree or at feasts in gilded fairy palaces. Not many people ever see a fairy palace. Those who are transformed into a tiny fairy and allowed to walk through the golden streets of the fairy kingdom never come back to normal, mortal life. They are so delighted with the way things are done, they simply stay. Now the trooping fairies delight in company, while the solitary fairies avoid large gatherings, preferring to be left by themselves and separate from one another.

"Fairies exist all over the world. In Ireland they are the s-i-d-h-e," he spelled it out. "It's pronounced *shee*, a name retained from the olden days. In a group they are the *'daione sidhe'* or fairy people. Some say that they get their name *'Aes Sidhe'* which means folk of the *'sidhe'* meaning hillock or mound from the large sidh or mound they inhabit; but others claim that the mounds got their name from the fairies' habitation of them. Who knows, *querida*? Now don't look at me like that. The banshee might be hiding away beside the road, keeping watch on me, so I must use an endearment occasionally," he whispered conspiratorially again.

"The trooping fairies are found living in the bushes & circles of stones that crop up all over Ireland. They're called the fairy raths. The fairy raths crop up in pastures all over Ireland, and the farmers never plow them up for fear of disturbing the fairies who live there & bringing bad luck upon themselves.

"Fairies are said to be very beautiful, with long yellow hair and perfect delicate forms. Just like you *a ghra*," he said without looking at her but feeling the wrath of her glare. Maybe some of the fire she was shooting would either keep her warm or melt the snow around them as they walked. If the bare branches of the trees began to sprout leaves he'd know there was indeed a banshee around and that Ellie's temper had brought spring into the middle of a very early winter.

He continued. "They love milk and honey and drink flower

nectar as their fairy wine. The fairies can assume any form and can make horses out of straw. They have the power to affect human life, especially unbaptized children. Fairies also love music, often luring mortals into an eternal dance with their piping and singing. And that's when they transform them into a creature of their own size and take them away to live forever in their gilded palaces."

"Is that all? Tell me, have you been baptized?" Ellie asked. Was that really the turn in the road up ahead? Had they come so far?

"Of course, within minutes of my birth so the fairies wouldn't cart me away to their palace. Even though I was the second son, my father didn't want to lose me forever," Colum said. They'd reached the fork in the road. He spied a dead fallen where they could sit a few minutes to catch their breath and have a bit of cold potatoes and roasted rabbit. He hoped it would carry them the rest of the way down the mountain.

"So what do men fairies look like?" She gratefully brushed the snow from the log beside the road and sat down. Never had her feet hurt so badly or been so cold for so long. Her toes were numb in spite of the stockings and good solid boots.

He opened his saddlebags and brought out the two rabbits, handing her one and tearing a leg off the other for himself. "I'll tell you more on the way down this mountain, *a ghra*," he said.

"You can stop that silly talk right now," she told him.

"And chance getting caught up in the banshee's spell? No thank you," he said, pulling the wool back over his mouth, both to hide the grin and for the warmth.

After they'd eaten and rested for fifteen minutes, he picked up the saddle and she stood up, suppressing a groan. Six more miles. At least four hours as slow as they had to travel in the snow. She had to endure it to prove to him that she could so there was nothing to do but put one cold foot in front of the other and hope her eyelids didn't freeze shut.

"Now the men fairies look like small old men," Colum began again, hopefully to pass the time for her. "Daddy told me the only ones he'd seen were about two feet tall and most usually dressed like shoemakers, with a cocked hat and a leather apron. According to Daddy, leprechauns are aloof, unfriendly, live alone, and pass the time making shoes. You see, the leprechauns cannot tolerate slothfulness. They must be at something even if they do possess a hidden pot of gold. Treasure hunters can often track down a leprechaun by the sound of his shoemaker's hammer. If caught, he can be forced to reveal the whereabouts of his treasure, but the captor must keep their eyes on him. If the captor's eyes leave the leprechaun, he vanishes and all hopes of finding the treasure are lost."

"Your father didn't really see one. Did he?" Suddenly the story was so real she wondered if the cold was affecting her brain if she was beginning to believe in such folderol.

"I never questioned my Daddy," Colum said seriously. "If he said he saw a two foot man and a blond haired wispy-waisted fairy woman, who was I to question him? I wasn't there when he kissed the Blarney Stone, nor when he saw the leprechauns, either."

"Then what is it about this banshee you keep mentioning. What gives her so much power she can make you have bad luck?" Ellie asked. Anything to keep him talking so she wouldn't think about the cold seeping through the layers and into her very soul.

"Oh, now *a ghra*, banshee is just a word for a fairy woman. Her sharp cries and wails are also called keen. The wail of a banshee pierces the night, its shrill notes rising and falling like the waves of the sea, somewhat like the wind whistling through the trees even as we walk. It's a haunting sound that pierces the soul to the very pits and strikes fear into the hearts of even six foot Irishmen. Because the noise of keening always announces a mortal's death. She is solitary woman fairy, mourning and forewarning those only of the best families in Ireland, those with most ancient Celtic lineage, whose names begin with Mc like McMath or McInnis or those with the first letter being O like O'Connor or O'Malley. My daddy's mother was an O'Connor so that puts him right in there with the highest kings. Each banshee has her own mortal family and out of pure love she follows the old race across the ocean to distant lands. Her wails or keen can be heard in America and England, wherever the true Irish have settled.

"When a member of the beloved race is dying, she paces the dark hills or even the flatlands of Texas about his house. She can be seen easily if you believe in the fairies. She's got silver-gray hair streaming to the ground and a white cloak of a cobweb-looking stuff clinging to her tall thin body. Her face is pale, her eyes red with centuries of crying.

"White Lady of Sorrow some people call her, and Lady of Death. Unseen, banshees attend the funerals of the beloved dead. Although, sometimes she can be heard wailing, her voice blending in with the mournful cries of others, it's only the sharpest of ears that can pick out the keening of a banshee. If you are very quiet and listen hard at an Irish wake you can tell the difference between her wailing and the mourning of mere mortals, though."

Ellie shivered and it had nothing to do with the cold. She wondered what it would be like to have had five brothers and a sister and live in a household where the Irish father told such wonderful stories. Did the Mexican mother tell her own stories, too? Someday she'd have to ask Colum about that.

No she wouldn't.

Because Colum Sullivan would go home and marry either one of those strange sounding words, a sweetheart in Irish, or a Mexican. He'd never be interested in a woman from the wrong side of the war who had an English mother. The Irish and the English were as different as the north and south. Neither mixed, and why was she thinking about trying to accomplish something impossible like that anyway. Her brain must surely be frozen solid.

Chapter Five

The road, barely wide enough for a small buggy, twisted and turned back on itself regularly. The Irish and Mexican garb he'd sewn for her had kept the worst of the cold at bay but it had begun to squeeze through by the time they reached the foot of the mountain. She could never remember being so cold, not even during the nights she spent in total fear chained to the wall in the cabin. Then she'd been stunned and floating in and out of reality. Now she was fully awake and the icy fingers of the wind gripped her beneath all the layers of clothing.

Sometime in late afternoon they reached the bottom of the mountainous road only to find a river on their right. The width of it caused Colum great concern. If there wasn't a bridge, how would they ever get across the thing? The first flakes of wet snow peppered against his face. Snow and sleet mixture, the wet flakes sticking to the exposed skin on his eyes and upper face, the sleet stinging as the wind tried to pierce his skin with it.

Colum fought fatigue. The saddle weighed six hundred pounds and gained weight by the minute—or so it seemed. Texas and a nice fall day was an eternity away. He put his oldest brother's face in his mind and kept putting one foot in front of the other. When he got home Patrick had a whipping coming, and Colum would be the one who destroyed his brother's good looks. If he didn't, at least Patrick would think twice before he invited some newspaper reporter home with him again. Patrick and his Irish generosity lay at the foundation of all Colum's problems. He invited Raymond Pierce home to stay at the ranch while the big eastern newspaper reporter worked up stories about the reconstruction of Texas after the war. Raymond took a shine to their little sister, Douglass, who ran off with him thinking they were eloping. Colum and Flannon were sent to bring her home, and when they arrived at the farm in Love's Valley, they found their baby sister had fallen in love with Monroe. Now Colum didn't have a thing against Monroe, liked the man even. But it was that sequence of events that brought him to be walking down a snow-covered mountain path with a wide river on one side, carrying his saddle and freezing half to death.

It was all Patrick's fault once it was traced back, and that's who was going to get his nose bloodied as soon as Colum stepped out of the saddle in DeKalb, Texas. He wasn't even going to hug his older brother until he'd gotten in the first hit. *Whip Patrick. Then go hug Momma and Daddy. Check on Grandpa and Grandma. Find the other brothers and hug them, then go back, pick Patrick up out of the dirt, take him in the house and clean up his face, and then hug him.* After all an Irishman didn't carry a grudge forever.

The wind used the bare limbs of the trees to play a haunting music that danced around Ellie's shoulders with the silent snow and sleet mixture. Why did winter have to arrive so early this year? There had been years when it didn't snow until Thanksgiving and a few when it didn't hit this hard until almost Christmas time. But, oh no, the very year she was kidnapped and had to walk out of the pits of Blacklog Valley was the year winter pushed fall into oblivion and arrived in October. What was it she'd told Colum? That the snow wouldn't be a lasting thing this early? Well, she was sure enough wrong. With cold this piercing and snow still falling, they'd be lucky to see bare ground before Easter.

Just a few more miles, maybe only one and she'd at least be inside a building of some kind where warmth could be found. She listened carefully to the echoes of the strange sounds flowing up and down the mountain side, and there amongst it was the high pitched wail of keening. The banshee woman Colum had told her about was wailing. Was it for Colum? Oh, dear Mary, mother of Jesus, what would she do if Colum were to drop dead with his saddle on top of him?

She listened more intently. There it was again. A high-pitched whine inside her head. Turning quickly to her left, she checked to see if Colum was still trudging along beside her. His eyes were weary and his face drawn with the cold journey, but he didn't look dead and he was still upright. Ellie told herself she wasn't Irish so the foreboding couldn't be for her own soul. Maybe since the banshee thought she was Colum's sweetheart, though, she would wail for her as well as Colum. The noise intensified and the clouds dropped from the heavens right in front of Ellie. Everything was gray and spinning in circles.

Colum took two steps forward before he fully comprehended that Ellie wasn't beside him. When he turned back to tell her to keep up, she was in a heap on the ground. He tossed the saddle from his shoulder and laid a hand on her neck. There was a strong pulse. She wasn't dead but simply fainted from exhaustion and cold. He gathered her into his arms, amazed at how light she was, and plodded on.

Around the very next bend in the road, there in the gray mist and falling snow was a building with a sign in the front proclaiming it to be some kind of church. "Praise and hallelujah," he mumbled through frozen lips. "If only the door is open, we'll have a refuge."

The door offered no resistance when he tried it, swinging open to reveal a small church with a center aisle flanked by two sides of pews. He carried Ellie all the way to the front where he spied the pot-bellied stove and laid her gently on the first pew. Then he hurriedly went about the business of making a fire. Wood lay in the grate beside the stove and a fire had already been readied inside when he opened the door. A tin box with only a small bit of rust on the lid held matches. In a few minutes the fire raged and began to warm the small church.

"Did the banshee get me?" Ellie mumbled, but she didn't open her eyes.

"No, the cold did," Colum carefully slipped the wet poncho over her head and laid it across the next pew to dry. "Can you sit up?"

"I don't think so. I think I can still hear the banshee wailing and moaning," she whispered. Where was the heat coming from? *Had the sun come out,* she wondered. Warmth was oozing into her face. Wonderful heat. She opened one eye barely a slit and the first thing she saw was the big, round stove. How on earth had Colum gotten that out to the mountain side?

"That'd just be the trick of the mind," Colum told her. "You fainted dead away back there a ways and I carried you inside this church. We'll be warm in a little while."

"Church?" Both her eyes popped open. They'd made it to civilization. She hadn't died. It wasn't the banshee crying for her or Colum.

"Yes, ma'am, a church. Now can you sit up so I can remove the Leine-and-Brat? They're wet from the knees down and we need to dry them out," he said.

She wobbled but she stayed in a seated position long enough for him to remove her wet things, her boots and stockings and even the trousers, which were damp to the knees also. She leaned heavily against his shoulder while he pulled the pants down and laid them with the other garments on the back of the pew. Finished, he tilted her back carefully to stretch out on the pew again.

"The fire will warm the church in a few minutes. Before I

get these wet things off me, I'm going back for my saddle," he told her.

"Mmm," she murmured, cold being chased away by the heat. All she wanted to do was sleep. Maybe for a whole week, cuddled up next to a fire in a nice clean building. She didn't care if he walked all the way back to Blacklog Valley for his precious saddle. Just before she drifted off to sleep she remembered something he'd said about burying her before he'd give up that saddle. What had changed his mind? The question was answered in her dreams of a dark-haired, brown-eyed Irishman with skin the color of coffee with lots and lots of fresh cream. Even in his bravado, he wouldn't leave her to die for his saddle.

Colum retraced his footsteps to the place where his saddle was already collecting a thick layer of snow, dusted it off and after two tries, got it to his shoulder again. By the time he reached the church he was panting, sucking in cold air and dampness into his lungs. He'd be lucky if he survived this trip without a dose of pneumonia himself. Leaving the saddle just inside the back door of the church, he went to the front to check Ellie. The whole trip couldn't have taken more than half an hour, but still she might have died in that length of time.

A quick check of her pulse let him know she was alive but sleeping soundly. She'd curled up in a ball on her left side, facing the onslaught of heat pouring from the stove. Using her arm for a pillow, her blond braid hanging to the floor, she'd never looked prettier. A rosy glow appeared in her cheeks even as he watched her sleep and he was reminded again of the fairies. If there were such creatures and they ever found Ellie walking alone in the forest, they would take her away to the fairy rafts beneath the earth, turn her into one of them and keep her forever. As lovely as she was, she might truly become royalty amongst them in their palaces.

He looked his fill, then stripped out of his own wet clothing, pulled his saddle to the front of the church and using it for a pillow, stretched out on the floor right in front of the blazing stove. Nothing had ever felt so good as that heat. Not one blessed thing. He turned toward Ellie so she'd be the first thing he saw when he awoke and fell asleep.

Ellie awoke clear-minded and yet there was a presence in the darkened church. The flicker of a light coming from the doorway, heavy footsteps up the center aisle, a gasp when the light was beside her. She looked up into the stern face of a man wearing a heavy black coat and carrying a candle in one hand.

"And who might you be? Some wanton woman Satan has left in my holy church to tempt me?" he asked in a booming voice.

Colum awoke from the floor right at the man's feet, his pistol in his hand and cocked before he was even fully awake.

At the sound of the gun, the man whipped around and looked down. "Ah, so it's two of you disgracing and tainting the Lord's house of worship? Get out of my church. I'll not have a wanton woman layin' on the front pew in nothing but her underwear. Nor a man doing the same. What gave you the right to start a fire and make yourselves at home in my church, anyway?"

"We were stranded. We'll be going as soon as we are dressed," Colum put his gun away.

"Yes, you will," the preacher said. "My church is desecrated. I'll have to wipe down all the pews to get your filth from it. You don't sound like you are from here, either. What are you? One of those misplaced, sorry Rebels?"

"Yes, I was a Confederate," Colum slipped into his pants and threw the Leine over his head.

"Oh, my sweet Lord and savior, you are a monk to boot. I shall have to pray the whole night through. A rebel and a Catholic monk, both desecrating my church," the man whispered angrily. "God won't even bless my service tomorrow with His presence if He realizes there's been Catholic heathen in here and one of those sorry southerners, too."

"You are radical," Ellie said, slipping her legs into the pants Colum tossed her way.

"And a woman who dresses like a man and has the nerve to call me a radical," the preacher had already began to intone and put his hands together in prayer. "My holy eyes can not look upon you anymore. I shall begin my prayers now," he said, kneeling in front of the altar and raising his eyes toward the ceiling, and praying loudly for God's saving grace and the blood of the Lamb to cleanse his church before services the next morning.

Colum and Ellie both dressed quickly. Colum picked up the saddle and they were about to open the back door when it swung inward and there stood a woman dressed from head to foot in black. She grabbed her heart when she saw Colum and Ellie before her and heard the loud prayers of her husband at the front of the church.

"'Scuse us, ma'am," Colum nodded respectfully. They were entitled to their belief. He'd just fought a war with that principle in mind. But it sure was taxing to be called the things that preacher had pronounced upon his Irish head. If he hadn't been raised to respect all kinds, the preacher man might have been preaching his sermon the next morning through a broken nose.

"Who are you?" she asked breathlessly, her beady little eyes drawing into mere slits, and the wrinkles across her forehead deepening.

"Just two weary travelers who seem to have brought God's wrath down upon your husband's head," Colum said.

"Where are you going?" she asked.

"To Allenport or Mount Union," Colum answered.

"Allenport is closer. It's only a mile right up this road," she whispered.

"Got a livery stable or a stage station?" Ellie asked.

"Livery stable this side of town. You can't miss it," she said. "Now go before he sees me talking to you."

Ellie nodded. Outside the clouds had passed even though the snow was still just as deep. Stars twinkled in the midnight blue sky like diamonds strewn over a nearly black piece of velvet fabric. Wasn't that just her luck? They'd trekked down the mountain on the day before the sun had a possibility of appearing.

"One mile," Colum said, hungry but refreshed from the rest and warmth. After what they'd already done, it seemed nothing in comparison, even in the dark. He'd rent a buggy and drive carefully by the light of the moon. By first light, he'd have Ellie back in the arms of his sister, Douglass, and the rest of the family. He'd love to be able to say that by the next morning he'd be on his way back to Texas. But that wasn't happening. Not now. Not until spring when the stage coaches and passes between the mountains reopened. Another winter in the mountains. *Yes, sir, Patrick is in for a good one.*

"I can walk a mile," she said. "Will we go on tonight?"

"Of course," he said. "There ain't nothing in this world could keep me from going to Love's Valley tonight."

An hour later they found the livery with the owner closing the doors.

"Luck of the Irish," Colum grinned at Ellie. "Another five minutes and we would have had to go further on and roust him out of bed to rent a buggy and horse."

"Evenin'," the man said. "What might you two be doin' out on a night like this?"

"Good evenin', sir," Colum said. "We're looking to rent a rig to take us over to Shirleysburg and into Love's Valley."

"Sorry, son. Can't do it," the man shook his head violently. "The sun has gone down. Until Monday mornin' when the sun comes up, 'tis the Lord's time. 'Twould be a sin to make profit on the Lord's Day."

"Another radical," Ellie murmured under her breath.

"I see," Colum said. "You cannot make profit on the Lord's Day?"

"That's what I just said. Would you be deaf as well as a southerner?" The man asked testily. "And is that a man or a woman walking with you?"

"It's a woman," Ellie said loudly.

"And what would you and the wife be doing walking, and you carrying along a saddle?" he asked.

"I'm not . . ." Ellie started but Colum butted in.

"Our horse died. Fell in a hole and I had to shoot him. We're looking for lodging or for a rig, but if you have neither, we'll walk on. How much farther is it to Mt. Union? Would they have a rig there?" Colum asked.

"I wouldn't be much of a Christian man if I let a poor woman walk on a night like this, now would I? But I wouldn't be much of one either if I made profit on the Lord's Day," he said, rubbing his jaw.

"Where's that Blarney Stone when we need it?" Ellie mumbled.

"Well now," Colum rubbed his own jaw. "Way I see it is that if you were to simply loan a couple in dire straits the use of one of your rigs, and that person just happened to leave a few coins under the front seat when he finished with the use of it, then it wouldn't be charging the fellow, now would it?"

"I don't think that's addressed in the Good Book," the man said. "How many coins would I happen to find when I came to claim my rig on Monday morning? And of course you wouldn't be needing to take it until first light. I couldn't even let you borrow it until then seeing as how the Lord would strike me dead if I was the cause of loaning a rig that caused your wife's death."

Colum sighed and Ellie set her jaw in anger.

"I suppose you would find a good sum, right there under the front seat of your rig and you could find both in the livery stable in Shirleysburg on Monday morning. But it's a moot question, isn't it? Because my wife," he almost choked on the word, "and I have no place to stay until morning."

"There's a nice warm room at the back of the livery. The fire is still going and banked to keep the embers until morning. There'd be only one bed. Use it myself when my own wife is out of sorts," the man said. "But . . ." he left the word hanging.

"But you cannot let us have the room because that would be making a profit on the Lord's Day?" Colum finished for him.

"But I might loan you the room and find a few coins left beneath the pillow on Monday morning," the man said cheerily.

"Hallelujah," Ellie said.

"Oh, a lady of the faith, I see," the man smiled and reset his hat on top of a mop of gray hair. "It's a fine room with clean linen. No bugs. Can't abide filth. Cleanliness is next to godliness, you know. Will I be seeing the two of you in the church tomorrow morning before you take your leave?"

"Which one?" Ellie asked.

"The one just up the road about a mile. Good Reverend Benson preaches a fine sermon. Hellfire and brimstone. Keeps you right on the edge of your seat and out of the clutches of Satan for a whole week," he said.

"I don't think we'll be having the good pleasure," Colum said. "The lady here has a need to be home in a hurry."

"Too bad," the man said. "Now go right on in and make yourselves comfortable. I don't suppose you'd want to put a few dollars in my hand now? Not for a deposit like I normally charge for the rig and the room, but more like a fine contribution to the church tomorrow morning."

"Give the man whatever he wants," Ellie said out of the side of her mouth. "If this isn't the biggest crock of horse manure I've ever had to listen to. Why doesn't he just charge us and get it over with?"

"And what did the little wife say? I missed that?" the man asked as he palmed the bills Colum laid in his hands.

"She was giving thanks to have found such a charitable Christian man on our travels. She was remembering the inn where our Lord and savior was brought into the world and thanking the Father that you have found it in your heart to give us such a consideration," Colum said.

Ellie sighed deeply. Colum must've wrapped his arms around the Blarney Stone and quite literally kept his lips sealed to it for hours.

"I'm just glad you found me when you did," the man said. "Use the rig tomorrow morning that's right inside the door. Horse in the first stall. He knows his business on snow. And don't let me be coming back here tonight and finding you gone. Should that happen, I'd be honor bound to call the sheriff and report my rig stolen. First light is early enough to be taking a wife on to Shirleysburg. Especially one who is expecting a baby."

Ellie almost choked.

"I knew that was the case when she thought of Jesus being born in the manger," the man grinned again. "Some old folks can't be fooled. I'm one of them."

"We'd be a thankin' you," Colum said, a flush creeping up the back of his neck in spite of the bitter night air.

"Did I hear a bit of Irish there, son?" the man asked.

"Yes, sir, you did. On my father's side. The Sullivans. His mother was an O'Connor," Colum said, hoping that didn't keep them from having the room.

"Well, now how's that for a fine evening? I'm Seamus O'Malley. Two Irish men sharing the same space and neither of them Catholic. How's that for a miracle? And folks think there's no more miracles. Well, you two have a good night and I'll be riding over to Shirleysburg on Monday morning to retrieve my rig. I'll look for that bag under the seat, now."

"And you will find it," Colum said with a smile. He'd go to confession soon as he got a chance and do all the Hail Mary's the father told him to do for lies, both real and of omission. But tonight his smooth Irish tongue had wrangled them a place to sleep and a means of escape at first light.

"Should've known. It takes one to know one," Ellie said, stomping through the straw-covered floor of the livery to the door toward the back.

"Blarney. Pure blarney. I didn't hear you piping up and saying that you weren't of that condemning faith and saying you were a Catholic, now did I?" Colum followed close behind.

"I couldn't have uttered a word after that comment about me being . . . well, you know," she said, throwing open the door.

The room was barely bigger than a two-hole outhouse but true to the livery keeper's word, the tiny stove in the corner kept it very warm. A table with a pitcher of fresh water took up one corner. A multi-colored quilt covered the bed and when Ellie threw back the covers there were clean sheets and two big fluffy pillows under the quilt.

He carefully unloaded his saddle beside the door.

"Coffee!" he exclaimed when he picked up the pot from the top of the stove. "Half full. Worth every lie I could tell, ain't it?"

He grabbed two tin mugs and filled them, drinking deeply before he set his down on the washstand beside the water pitcher. He pushed on the bed. "Feather. Heavenly feathers. Which side do you want?"

"What are you talking about, Colum Sullivan. I want the whole bed. I'm not sleeping with you, and that's a fact," she said.

"Oh, but *a ghra* you are sleeping with me. That's all we will do and we'll do it in our undergarments. I'll even put the saddle between us if you like, but I'm sleeping in that bed. It's plenty wide enough for two people," he said.

"Don't you call me those strange Irish or Mexican endearments," she said. "I could sleep sitting up in a drafty old outhouse. So I'll take the floor."

"Your choice," he said, stripping the poncho over his head and hanging it on one of the many pegs on the wall. "I assure you though, you are surely not my type and I'm too tired to molest you even if you were."

That stung. Calling her sweetheart and darling in foreign tongues, then insulting her like that. "Well, I assure you, Mr. Smooth Talking Irishman, you are not my type either, and I'm not too tired to put both your eyes out if you did try to molest me. Is there any food in those saddlebags. I'm starving."

"Got a couple of hard tack biscuits I tossed in this morning and a bit of jerky left," he said.

"Give me some of it," she ordered without even using the word *please*. He didn't deserve it after that remark. He wasn't a gentleman of any caliber or he'd sleep on the floor and give her the bed. She jerked the poncho over her head in anger, unbelted the Brat and took off the Leine. When they were on hooks, she removed the pants and her boots and stockings. His shirt hung down past her hips and besides he'd seen her in less so the modesty most usually draped firmly around her disappeared.

She sat down on the edge of the feather mattress and sighed. Chewing on the hard biscuit he'd made for supper the night before, she gave some serious thought to sleeping on the bed after all.

But she couldn't.

Why not? she argued with herself. Colum had promised not to molest her and she had no doubt about how tired he was, because she'd walked every step that he had that day and she was that tired, too. Well, almost every step, she argued again. He had carried her from the place where she fell to the church. Besides they'd slept no more than two feet apart the whole time in the cabin. Her next to the fire and him close enough away he could have reached out and touched her at any time. He'd been a gentleman there so why did she think he'd be any different now. And he had said she wasn't his type, hadn't he?

By the time they'd eaten enough to keep body and soul together their eyes were drooping. The floor looked hard and uninviting. Ellie considered the bed. Her reputation was already in tatters, torn apart by a man of far less caliber than Colum Sullivan. She looked down at the wooden floorboards. They were clean and she could use the quilt, leaving him the rest of the covers.

She set her full, sensuous mouth in a firm line. Be damned to the floor.

"I'll take the side next to the wall," she said. "And don't wake me at first light. We can make it to Shirleysburg in less than three hours. There's a little station about half way there where we can get a bite of breakfast." She crawled across the bed and snuggled down between clean sheets, resting her head on a soft pillow, and was asleep before he could answer.

"Yes, ma'am," he whispered, easing his own tired body in next to hers, being very careful not to touch her. *And I promise I will go to confession for all the lies,* he told himself. *Especially for that one about not being attracted to Ellie. Lord, a man would have to be seven days in the grave not to be attracted to someone who looks so much like a fairy. But I'd be crazy to ever let her know it. She'd reject me before a gnat could blink twice on a hot Texas day. I'm a Confederate. I'm Irish and I'm Mexican. Either one would get me thrown out on my ear. Put all three together and it's a pure disaster. No, I'll do good to steer clear of this beauty until I can drag my heart back home to Texas where I belong.*

Chapter Six

True to Seamus's word, the horse did seem to know his business on the snow packed road from Allenport to Shirleysburg. The big black animal kept a steady pace but not a fast one. Lost in deep thoughts, Ellie was silent. Everything in her world had done a hundred and eighty degree turn around then a flip-flop upside down in the past days, emotions included. What she'd trusted in, believed in, had failed her miserably. That which she could put no trust in, could never believe in had stood beside her faithfully. Nothing made a bit of sense.

The brisk morning air bit into Colum's unshaven face but the sun warmed his soul and for that he was grateful. If he and Ellie had stayed one more day in the cabin they could have walked with the blessing of the sun's rays on their faces, but hind sight was the only perfect vision in the world. Who was he to know the sun would hide behind the clouds all day or that it would come out the next day? Could have been that there would have been another foot of snow for them to trudge in all the way down that mountain. Ellie hadn't talked much since they left Allenport, but then she was going home today and nothing else could go wrong. She'd survived the whole ordeal with stamina and strength

64

that surprised him. He hoped she hadn't made it through only to fall apart when back in her home and in the arms of her family.

He'd seen that happen in the war. Men, who fought valiantly, even after they were wounded. Stood their ground and kept fighting until the enemy retreated. Then when they were back at the campsite, they fell apart. Hands shaking, eyes wide and set, whole body trembling. Maybe Ellie was just waiting to get home so she could do the same. Only time would tell.

"Right around the bend here is the stage station where we can get something to eat. I hope they've made gravy this morning. Real milk gravy and biscuits," Ellie said, breaking the silence.

"Oh, and her English royalty wishes for something with a little milk rather than a nice bowl of stew?" he raised a black eyebrow.

"If you ever call me that again, I'll bury you under the horse manure pile out back of the barn. I'm sick to death of it. I don't call you your Irish King or your Mexican Lord or anything like that so you can cut out the name calling right now," she said, eyes boring into his.

"Well, well, the lass has a temper this morning. Rest assured *querida* I shall be careful what I call you from now on. I would certainly not wish my bones to rest beneath a Yankee manure pile for all eternity. The fairies would never retrieve my soul from such a place. Is that the station, then?" He pointed to a building on the side of the road.

"That's it," she said. "We've stopped there a few times, Indigo and me, when we've taken the stage over to Mt. Union to my lawyer's office."

"I see, and why would you need a lawyer?" He stopped the rig and hopped down.

"I'd say that's none of your business," she said, coolly. Before she could throw the covers from her legs, he was standing beside her, his hand out to help her down. He'd already removed his gloves. She wasn't prepared for the shock when her bare hand touched his. Their fingers had brushed against each other several times during the days in the cabin and he'd carried her to the church, but she never remembered a jolt like that to her system. It must have something to do with the fact that her own hand was warm from being wrapped in the lap quilts, and his was cold from removing his gloves on the way around the rig.

"Well, well, what have we here?" The man inside the station said in a big, booming voice. "Wasn't expecting no travelers on a day like this. Why, Miss Hamilton, is that you under all that garb? Can't say as I've ever seen you wearing such things before."

"Good morning, Mr. Secrest. I don't suppose you have seen me like this but a lady will wrap up in most any old thing to keep warm, you know. Would you have some breakfast ready?" she asked.

"Wife just made a little bit in case of an emergency and then she went on back to the house," he said. "Got some corn meal mush ready to fry, a small pot of gravy and a pan of biscuits. Interested?"

"In all of it," Ellie said. "This is my . . ." she stopped dead in her physical tracks as well as the mental ones. How did she introduce Colum?

He waited, a grin on his face and no offer of help to fetch her out of the embarrassing predicament she was in. Did she say friend? Rescuer? Part of the family? Or Rebel? Irish rogue? Mexican scoundrel?

"This is Colum Sullivan. He's a brother to Monroe's new wife, Douglass. Guess you've heard about Monroe up and marrying the Texan? And this is Mr. Secrest," Ellie spoke quickly to cover her own nervousness.

"I'm right glad to meet you, sir," Colum extended a hand which was met with a firm shake.

"Likewise," the man said. "Only call me Thomas. Mr.

Secrest sure makes me feel old. Seems like I ought to see my father standing behind me."

"Well done *querida*," Colum whispered so low that only she could hear it.

"I'll just be a minute," Thomas hurried off to the back room that served as a kitchen to slice the corn meal mush and fry it. Thank goodness there was plenty of maple syrup to go along with it. "Heard that you'd done jilted Oscar Wright. Then got word just yesterday that you'd been kidnapped. That the truth?"

"Yes, it is," Ellie raised her voice as she slipped off the poncho, the Brat, and finally the Leine, and warmed her hands in front of the big, raging blaze going in an open fireplace. "I did break it off with Oscar. Should've seen from the beginning that he was only interested in my money. Two men, named Turley and Alvie, kidnapped me the next morning when I went to the barn to clean the horse stables. They tied me up in a cabin and came near to starving me. Left me for dead. Colum rescued me."

"Humpph," Thomas peeped around the door to find, much to his surprise, the very prim and proper Elspeth Hamilton wearing men's clothing under all that strange-looking, dull-colored clothing. "Wonder you ain't dead. Turley might be stupid but he would've killed you in a minute. He and Alvie are mean ones, they are. Never did have no schoolin' or such. Just two mean old boys. You want syrup or jam with this mush?"

"Both," Ellie said.

"So you seen anything of Turley or Alvie?" Colum asked when Thomas set the plates on a small table in the corner beside the fire. He'd finally figured out what didn't fit in the puzzle this whole time. He'd mulled it over time and time again in the cabin and even while he and Ellie rode in from Allenport to the stage station that morning. Something just didn't make a bit of sense in the whole picture. Now he knew. Turley and Alvie might have done the dirty work, but neither of them were smart enough to have written that ransom note. Colum had seen it, held it with his own hands, and read it many times. It'd been written by someone with an education, a flair with the pen as well as the prose. And Colum was pretty sure he knew who had ridden away from the cabin that morning he'd shot his own horse.

Thomas drug up a chair from a nearby table and sat with them. "Nope, ain't seen hide nor hair of them in more'n two weeks. What did they do to you? That's quite a bruise on your face."

"Beat me every day in some form. Either slapping me or kicking me. That's just one of many bruises Turley left on me," she said quietly.

"He ain't much of a man. Haul off like that and beat on you. Just like his sorry old daddy used to be. Beat up on his ma lots of times. Next time he comes through here I might put a little something in his food to make him sorry," Thomas said.

"Next time he comes through here, you just tell him Colum Sullivan has a bit of a squabble he'd like to settle with him. That is if the sheriff don't catch him beforehand," Colum replied as he dug into the breakfast with the gusto of a hungry hound after a full night of chasing Texas coons.

"You ain't heading for Shirleysburg now, are you?" Thomas asked. "Oops, plumb forgot your coffee. Some waiter I am. Wife usually does these chores for me but we wasn't expecting anyone in the forenoon at all. Thought we might have one stop on up toward evening time."

"Yes, we are. We've borrowed or rented or whatever you want to call it, that rig out there and we've just stopped for breakfast," Colum said.

"Then you've got a long stop ahead of you. Might near all day if you're lucky. If you ain't so lucky then you'll be sitting right here until tomorrow. Bridge is iced up solid over the Aughwick Creek. Ain't no way a little old rig like that one is going to get across it. Sun's out and come evening a stage might be able to get to the other side since it'd be heavier and have more horses to pull it, but right now the sheriff has put a block on both ends 'til it thaws out. Be a tragedy if someone's rig went over the side and into them icy waters. Be the death of them and a good horse," Thomas said, setting the hot pot of coffee in the middle of the table with one hand and dangling three tin cups from his fingers on the other.

"But it's just a short little bridge. We could cross it even in the snow," Ellie almost whined.

"Might be you could in the snow. Body could dust it off the sides. But that was some real freezin' rain and sleet that fell on us most of the day yesterday. Heard there was a layer three inches thick on the bridge. No, ma'am, sheriff won't let nothing but the evening stage across that bridge even if he's allowing that," Thomas said. "You might as well just get comfortable. You got a hankerin' for a nap, I could rent you a room upstairs for the rest of the day."

"This is fine," Ellie said. "Where are the old newspapers?"

"On the back table where I keep them all. Just be sure you put them all back nice and neat," Thomas said. "Now where is it you're from?" He filled the cups and turned toward Colum.

"North Texas. Little town called DeKalb. Raise some horses and cattle. Do a bit of ranching," Colum said.

"Well, ain't that something. What're you doing up here?" Thomas asked.

"Come to rescue that sister of mine only to find out she'd already been rescued," Colum chuckled.

"Sounds like a story to be told on a cold winter day when a body can't go nowhere anyhow. Reckon you'd be up for telling it if I keep the coffee hot and coming along when you need it?" Thomas asked.

"I might be persuaded to give you a little bit of the story," Colum grinned.

"Hmmmph," Ellie snorted. "Don't let him fool you, Mr. Secrest. He's loved on the Blarney Stone and can talk rings around any tale. I'm taking my coffee to that chair right there," she pointed to an upholstered chair beside the fire, "and I'm going to read every word in those papers. You two can entertain yourselves however you want."

Ellie attempted to block out the tale by reading all about McInnis's new baby girl, Bessie Mary, who'd been born the week before in Shirleysburg, according to the newest newspaper she'd found on the table. But before long she only pretended to read, keeping the paper in front of her face to hide the smiles and biting her tongue to keep from laughing as she listened intently to Colum's story of how he came to be in south central Pennsylvania during the winter of 1866.

She almost jumped out of her chair when he told about how Douglass had hoodwinked him and his brother Flannon by buying a ticket to some little town in Arkansas and they went off on a wild goose chase giving her a head start. That, only after she'd nearly been discovered in a general store when they'd walked within three feet of her and didn't even see her. He gave details and told how he'd felt during the whole trip, from his Irish temper wanting to strangle his defiant sister, to his better sense worrying that she might be dead.

Ellie held in giggles. She battled tears. When the story ended she wanted more. Couldn't Thomas ask a question or two so Colum would tell some more? Even a repeat of the fairy story wouldn't be so bad. But Thomas didn't. He slapped his leg, enjoyed the reprieve from a long dull morning and said that he was going up to the house to check on his wife and family. He offered to bring down some lunch from his wife's cook stove at no charge just to pay for the storytelling, and Colum thanked him.

Ellie focused her eyes on another newspaper. An older one brought across country from the western end of Tennessee. There'd been a horrible riot with people being killed. So resettling the country wasn't such an easy job after all, she thought, as she read on. And Monroe had been sent into hot pots of anger and fear just like that one in Memphis, Tennessee. Was it as bad in Galveston, Texas? A frown creased her brow and she worried through the story. Or worse yet, what was going on in Savannah, Georgia where Harry was until the end of summer. Or in Louisiana where Henry Rueben had been sent to help with the reconstruction. They'd both be home by fall, but if there were riots in those places their very lives could be in danger. Suddenly she feared for Monroe's two younger brothers and offered up a silent prayer for their safe return home.

"And what has you so upset, *querida?*" Colum asked from a new advantage, in the upholstered chair next to her. "Has the fashions gone to bustles again, or is there a shortage of velvet for the winter frocks?"

She could listen to that soft southern drawl with just a hint of Irish lilt all day, but be hanged if she'd let him know that. "If you must know, I was reading about that riot in Memphis and worrying my head off about Henry Rueben and Harry Reed. They would be Monroe's two younger brothers who are still working for the government even if the cursed war is over. Women can think beyond new dresses and fashions, you know. We have a brain the same size as yours and we are capable of using it," she snipped.

"Ah, *a ghra,* don't be angry with this son of a poor Irish potato farmer. I was just making light of the wrinkles so they'd disappear. Now they've deepened," he said.

"Stop calling me those words. I don't like 'her English royalty' or those other two either," she said.

"And what am I supposed to call you? Ellie or Elspeth?" he asked, amusement dancing across his handsome square face and settling into those light brown eyes that fascinated Ellie so much.

"You may call me Miss Hamilton," she said as cold as she could.

"Very well," Colum flipped out the newspaper and began to read, ignoring her. So it was to be on a formal basis from now on, was it? If that's what the lady wanted then that's what she would get for sure. No more fairy tales. No more telling of the journey from DeKalb, Texas where he left his family to search for his errant sister, only to have a blond-haired witch attack him and scratch his face. Only a business arrangement. If that's what she wanted, then he would deliver it. Far be it for him to push his intentions, even friendly ones, where they weren't wanted.

Thomas came back, bringing a quart of potato soup and a whole loaf of fresh bread from the oven, still steaming from the coating of sweet cream butter his wife had rubbed on it to keep the crust soft. He and Colum talked about the weather, the crops for the next spring, how the railroad would affect the stagecoach business, and whether or not the sun was doing its job of melting the ice on the Aughwick Creek bridge.

Ellie listened with one ear, loving the deep, resonant sound of Colum's voice, and ate the soup while letting her mind wander a bit when Colum wasn't talking. Why did that man bring out the worst in her? She never was so short with Oscar and he'd been a real skunk in the woods. With Colum, though, she said what she thought when it crossed her mind. She kept back nothing. If she agreed with him, so be it. If she disagreed, he could live with it.

Somewhat like the relationship she'd seen between Douglass and Monroe. Who'd have ever thought in their wildest dreams, Monroe, a staunch Union man, would come dragging home a Confederate wife from Texas of all places. Much less one who was mixed up with Irish and Mexican blood. Yet, there she was, arguing with him, making him toe the line and he walked around with a moony expression reserved for idiot men in love and little puppies.

Oscar never had that look in his eyes. Not one time. Looking back, she realized that the only time she saw anything remotely similar was when he talked about what they would do with her money after they were married. Until some man gazed on her like Monroe did when he looked at Douglass, she vowed she would never marry. And she'd never, ever walk around on eggshells trying to please a man again. They could take her for herself or they could simply go away. If one ever pulled a stunt like Oscar had done, she and Douglass would shoot him and bury him in the horse manure pile. Like Douglass had said, God wouldn't even lay the charge to their souls, as sorry as Oscar was.

The clock on the wall above the mantle struck four times just as the stagecoach pulled up in front of the station. Thomas came out of the back room where he'd been stacking supplies and opened the door. Only the driver and the man riding shotgun ambled in.

"Still colder'n a mother-in-law's kiss," the driver said, blushing scarlet when he realized there was a lady in the room. Even if she did wear men's pants, there was no doubt she was all woman with that fair skin and long, blond braid. "Beggin' pardon, ma'am. Don't think you're old enough to be a mother-in-law, but shoulda watched my words. Didn't see you there."

Ellie nodded, folded her paper neatly and stood up, stretching several hours worth of kinks from her back. "Is the bridge ready to cross?" she asked.

"Don't know. We were told to come this far and the sheriff would send a rider if we can get across. Seen him, yet?" the driver asked.

"Ain't seen nobody," Thomas said. "You two hungry?"

Before either of them could answer the door swung open again and a lone man hurried in, slamming the door behind him. "Been here long? The sheriff sent me to say the stage can cross if you get on down the road. Ice is pretty well melted and a couple of deputies will help you get 'er across. Road is slippery right up to the bridge. I come across right easy, leading my horse just to test it all. Reckon it'll take an hour or more to get there, across and into town. But that's better'n settin' here all night. I'm on my way home to Mt. Union so the sheriff asked me to deliver the message to anyone here at the station."

"Would you mind taking that rig out there home to the livery in Allenport? Be willin' to pay you to do so." Colum asked.

"Wouldn't mind at all. Won't cost you nothing though. Can't be charging for doing a Christian deed, especially on the Lord's day. I'll just tie my horse on behind and get on out of here. Good day to you all," he said and went out the door.

Colum followed close behind him, grabbing his poncho on the way out the door and slinging it over his head. "Wait a minute, I've got to put something in under the buggy seat. Promised the man who wouldn't rent it and loaned it to me that I'd leave something there so he wouldn't be making a profit on the Lord's day."

"That's Seamus. He's not taking no chances of going to hell, but he sure ain't one to pass up a dollar either," the man laughed. "I'll see to it that it's untouched so you won't be the subject of his prayers tonight."

"Whew," Colum wiped his brow in mock horror. "I'm beholden to you. What's your name in case I need to know it in the future."

"Curtis Mathias, from Mt. Union. I run a store on Shirley Street. Come see me if you're ever in town. You ain't from these parts are you?"

"Texas," Colum slipped money into a small sack he kept in his saddlebags and shoved it up under the buggy seat.

"Well, the war is over. Just don't bring it in my store," Curtis said.

"Thank you, sir," Colum told him and rushed back inside the station to get his saddle and the rest of his garments loaded.

The stage crossed the narrow bridge slowly but safely and Ellie breathed a huge sigh of relief. They'd rent a rig and be home not too long after dark. Now nothing really could go wrong. She'd lived through it all. She was on the right side of the Aughwick. Colum would continue to protect her the rest of the way home.

Colum leaned his head against the back of the seat. It was nice to have someone else drive while he opened his eyes just enough to study Miss Hamilton sitting across from him. What would it be like to kiss those lips? Would she melt like ice with the sun's warm rays pouring down upon it, or had she been scarred so badly by that dirty scoundrel that nothing would ever melt her heart? Did she hate him most because he had been a Rebel and they'd burned her house and cheated her out of years with her parents? Or did she hate him because he was an Irishman who everyone looked down upon? Or was it the Mexican blood that riled her?

Questions. Questions.

No answers.

Ellie felt his stare but in her newly found independence didn't even squirm once. She propped her shoulder into the corner and pretended to rest her eyes. She didn't need to keep them open to see Colum Sullivan. His image was forever branded on her brain. Those dark, brooding eyes, serious one minute, dancing with laughter the next. That handsome square chin. The mouth she wondered what would be like to touch with her lips. She knew it all because all of Colum haunted her dreams nightly.

But he was a fine southern gentleman who wouldn't have any use for a Yankee woman like her. Not only was she an unforgiving northerner but English as well, as he'd so often reminded her, and it didn't take a history book from the Shirleysburg Seminary for Ladies to know how the English and Irish got along. He'd be thinking she was too cold and uppity to suit his tastes. Not to mention the fact that she was tall and gangly, not a dark-haired beauty like his sister. In the summer if she wasn't careful her fair skin tended to freckle. He'd hate freckles, she just knew it without any further thought on the matter. He sure didn't like her sassy attitude these days, but that was something she didn't intend to ever change. Not for anyone. Especially a brown-eyed rebel with a deep Texas drawl.

So Colum would have to stay in her dreams like he did every night since he took the shackles from her legs. Too bad that in reality he couldn't take them from her heart. As it was, the fair-haired Yankee and the dark-haired Rebel would never be compatible.

Chapter Seven

Nothing was fair. Most especially not life that evening. Ellie felt like a pouting little girl who'd not gotten her way at a tea party and she didn't even feel guilty about it. She'd survived a week of the substance nightmares were made of, only to get into Shirleysburg so late that Cleatus Harris at the wagon yard and livery had already shut up shop. He and his family were at church and even a pouting child knew better than to march into the middle of the Sunday evening services, demanding Cleatus rent them a rig. By the time their preacher turned them loose it would be entirely too late to start out for Love's Valley, hence the pouting and the realization that they would have to spend the night in Shirleysburg.

Ellie and Colum marched stoically down the street to the Franklin Hotel. Colum had had his heart set on ending the job that very day, but his Irish luck had just plumb played out. Truth be told he didn't mind a night in the hotel, a room of his own, a nice soft bed to sleep in, but there was a very good chance that low-down snake, Oscar Wright was still in town. He might think he could wiggle his way back into her life after the kidnapping or else finish the job of killing her if Colum was right in what he'd figured out that morning.

77

Douglass had told him about how Ellie broke the engagement because the man was only interested in her money, but none of them had suspected for a minute that Oscar was the brains behind the kidnapping. At least not until Colum had heard Turley called stupid.

The ideal situation would be for Colum to sneak Ellie out of town before the man even knew she was around. Get her back into the bosom of the family in Love's Valley where Douglass, Indigo, and Mrs. Laura, not to mention Monroe and even Colum could keep Oscar out of Love's Valley. But Shirleysburg had one through street with houses on both sides. If anyone stopped by the restaurant and bar in the hotel lobby and the clerk mentioned Ellie's name, it would spread over town like wildfire on the Texas prairie.

Sure, and Colum wanted the job to be finished. Done. Deliver the merchandise to the front door and into Laura Hamilton's arms with Douglass and Indigo standing by to help out. From that point he would have nothing to do with the illustrious Miss Hamilton with the snooty ways. Lord save the man who fell in love with all that blond hair and blue eyes.

Ellie wanted to cry but there was no way Colum was going to see her shed even one tear. If she let one past the dam, the flood gates would come down and she'd bawl for hours. The only good thing about the fact they'd have to stay in town was that with such horrid weather there were no travelers so there shouldn't be any shortage of rooms in the hotel. Colum held the door open for her. She stomped inside, threw the hood from her head and stared the man behind the desk right in the eye. If he had a mind to insult the way she was dressed, she intended to unload a whole week's worth of pure mad upon his head.

"May I help you?" he asked without so much as a faint grin. A smart man, he recognized Miss Elspeth Hamilton the minute she threw back that hood. Oscar would pay him well for that bit of information. He'd come by just yesterday asking if the Rebel from out at Love's Valley had been seen in town. Had given the clerk a ten dollar gold piece to keep his eyes and ears open. If he saw either the Rebel or heard any news of Ellie Hamilton to let him know right away.

"We need two rooms for the night," Colum said so close behind her the warmth of his breath tickled the soft skin on her neck.

"Well, that's easy enough," the man said. "Number 201 for the lady. If you will sign right here, please. And 203 for the gentleman. And you would sign, too," he shoved the ledger in front of them.

Ellie dipped the pen in the ink bottle and signed her name with a flourish right beside the number 201.

Colum dipped the pen but looked closely at the ledger.

"I'd like 202 if it's available," Colum said, noting that there was no name on the line for that room.

"Sorry, sir. That one's already taken," the man didn't look up.

The hair on Colum's neck stood at attention. Who was in 202 or who was coming back to it?

"We'd like supper brought to the rooms, and baths," Ellie said, starting up the stairs.

"Anything special or just what the cook has in the kitchen?" the man asked.

"I'm not picky. Just bring food. And lots of it. Then the baths. Tubs, not just basins and lots of hot water," Ellie said without looking back. "Then would you send a messenger to my dressmaker, Mrs. Whitzel, across the street when she returns from her church services? I'll have a note ready to carry to her by the time you have my supper brought up."

"Yes, ma'am," the man said. "The cook has his son with him tonight. The boy can deliver the note, I'm sure. And the cook will have your food up in a few minutes." While the messenger was out he could go right on down the street to the room Oscar Wright had rented and deliver another note from the clerk, himself. Yes, sir, some nights it just paid a man to go ahead and work even though it was bound to be a slow evening.

Colum picked up the keys the clerk laid on the desk. "Here's yours," he handed one to Ellie and kept the other tightly in his hand.

When they reached the numbered doors, Ellie stopped in front of 201. She shoved the key into the door and turned but nothing happened. "Now what?" she said.

"Well, for starters, *querida,* you're trying to open the wrong door. He said you were in 203, remember?" Colum held up his key with 201 written on the tag hanging from it.

"He did not. I signed my name on 201," Ellie rolled her eyes at the endearment. *What did* querida *mean, again? Darling? Sweetheart?* Too tired to fight, she gritted her teeth and ignored his sarcasm. "He said *you* were in 203."

"What number is on your key?" Colum asked.

She turned it over and there in big print was 203. "I could've sworn he said 201. Not that it matters. The rooms are all probably just alike. I'll see you then in the morning." she said, going on down the hall to her room.

"Whew," Colum leaned against the back of the door. She must be tired not to demand the answers to a hundred questions, the first being why did he want her room? He might be wrong about Oscar. It could have been any one of a hundred or more other men who penned that note. But down deep, Colum didn't think so. Not with the timing. He stared at the soft bed, knowing he couldn't take a chance on even a thirty minute nap. It was going to be a long, long night. He'd gotten soft since the war. Time was he could stay up two nights snatching only bits of sleep here and there. He'd put all that behind him more than a year before or so he'd sworn when the war ended. Now, Miss Hamilton had brought it all about again. He longed to be home in Texas where there was nothing more dangerous than an unbroken horse or a rangy bull. At least he'd slept fairly well the night before. As well as a man could with a beautiful woman in bed with him and not even one toe was supposed to touch her.

Ellie shucked out of the extra layers of clothing once again, left them laying on the floor and tested the bed. Nice. Not as soft as the one in the livery at Allenport but still very nice. Clean sheets covered by a lovely patchwork quilt. A rocker beside the window caught her attention and she sunk into it, watching the stillness of the night. Stars twinkling, moon high in the sky. Not a soul on the streets. Pure quietness. A complete diametrical opposition to the storm tormenting her heart.

She was still sitting in silence when someone knocked on her door. She flung it open to find the hotel cook with a small table. "Oh, I was expecting to find Mr. Sullivan in this room. The clerk said he had this room and you had the other one, a couple of doors down. Not that it matters a bit. Supper is the same. Ham pot pie and lots of it just like he said you ordered. Bread baked since dinnertime today. A pot of tea and blueberry cobbler for dessert. I remembered that you preferred tea to coffee from when you and your cousin drop by for lunch on the days you do your shopping."

"It sounds wonderful," she said. "Thank you. Just set it inside the door."

"Of course," the cook said. "Clerk said you wanted a note delivered?"

"Oh, I forgot it." She crossed the room to the small desk, picked up a piece of paper from the top and penned a note to her dressmaker. Maybe she'd have something decent already sewn up that Ellie could purchase.

"I'll see to it that it is sent immediately. Got my son in the kitchen with me. His mother went to church but he begged off to keep me company. I'll send him over there," the cook said when she handed him the folded note.

Ellie repositioned the table of food right next to the window and pushed back the curtain so she could look outside

as she ate. Soon the church services would be finished and
at least she could see the people scurrying home to get out
of the cold. Sure enough people began to hurry home from
the church across and down the street a bit. The small boy
with her note slipped and slid across the icy street. Ellie
smiled at all the acrobatics he had to do to keep from land-
ing square on his hind end. In the melee of slinging his arms
about, her note went skittering all the way to the wooden
sidewalk. Ellie watched as he retrieved it and another piece
of paper that landed a few feet away. Her curiosity piqued,
she watched him closely as he gave Mrs. Whitzel her note
even before she opened the door to her small two-story
house. Then he carefully made his way down two doors to
the rooming house run by Florence Moser. Without knocking, he entered the front door and in a few minutes Ellie
could see two figures in one of the upstairs windows. The
lace curtains and half-drawn shade didn't allow her to even
make a guess as to who the boy handed the note to in that
room. Perhaps Colum had business with someone and sent
out his own note. Or whoever had the room between theirs
had sent a message across the street. A cold chill rippled
down her backbone. Something wasn't totally right and she
could feel it. She shook it off, chalking it up to a case of
nerves, and rightly so after the past two weeks.

By the time she'd finished off the pot of tea, the clerk had
drug in an oval bathtub, set it in the middle of the floor, and
filled it with warm water, making several trips to do so.
When he finished, Ellie tested the water, found it much to
her liking and was in the process of unbuttoning the shirt
Colum loaned her when she heard steps on the stairs and
then a gentle rap on her door. She opened it to find Mrs.
Whitzel with a question in her eyes.

"Did you have anything?" Ellie asked.

"I brought what I had that would fit you," she said, brush-
ing past Ellie into the room and closing the door behind her

at the same time. She laid an armload of clothing on the bed. "Oh, my dear, what has happened to your face?"

"It's a long story. I'll shorten it down best as I can while I look at what you have," Ellie said, holding up two skirts. Both serviceable. One blue and one purple. One shirtwaist with a floral design, leg-o-mutton sleeves and a high collar, which would match either skirt. A complete set of new under things and even a velvet cloak and matching hat of the deepest purple velvet.

"I'll take it all. Put in on my account and I'll settle it like I always do at the end of the month," Ellie said. "The shortened form of what happened to me is that right after Douglass and Monroe were married a couple of weeks ago, I broke my engagement to Oscar because I found out he was interested in my money, not me. The next morning, I was kidnapped, knocked unconscious and hauled over to a trapper's cabin in Blacklog Valley. Monroe's new wife, Douglass, sent her brother to rescue me, and that's the story."

"Oh, my dear," Mrs. Whitzel fumbled with her handkerchief. "The bruises are awful. I heard you'd broken it off with Oscar. He's playing the poor jilted groom. Says he doesn't know what got into you. That he loved you but honey, he's not sitting still. He's been seen the last couple of days paying court to the Widow Sudder. Did that evil man . . . the kidnapper . . . hmmm . . . hurt you in other ways?"

"No, he didn't. I was so sick by the time the week was over he just left me to die, chained to the wall of that cabin. Said the bears or wolves would eat the flesh from my bones before spring after I'd starved to death," Ellie said.

"Oh, my. Oh, my," Mrs. Whitzel wrung her hands and shuddered so hard that the gray bun at the nape of her neck shook. "I suppose I'll have to tell the Widow Sudder about it and she's not going to believe me. But it's my honor bound duty not to let her get mixed up with such a man. She's older than he is, you know, and it does look silly to see him paying court to her."

"You tell her whatever you want. Could be he's out for her money, too," Ellie said. "Thank you so much for bringing the clothes."

"Well, I must be going, child, before your bath water draws chilly. I'll see to the Widow knows right after breakfast in the morning. Let me know when you've a mind to have something else made for you. Good night," Mrs. Whitzel said, waving from the door as she closed it.

Ellie turned the key in the lock, laid it on the vanity and shucked out of the rest of her things. She sunk down into the bath water and sighed deeply. She'd never take such things as food, heat, and a bath for granted again.

Colum rushed through his supper and his bath and still nerves crawled on the back of his neck. He'd checked his watch at least a dozen times when at exactly ten thirty he heard the footsteps on the stairs. They stopped at the room between his and Ellie's and he heard a man swear in a deep voice when he had trouble finding the key hole in the darkened hallway. Colum pressed his ear to the adjoining wall and shut his eyes. The man dropped first one boot and then the other on the floor, rocked a while in the chair, mumbled a few words to himself and then according to the squeak of the bed springs, fell into bed.

Now, Colum could be wrong, but he hadn't been too many times in his life. He'd finally realized how right he was when the clerk just out and out lied to them about someone being in that room. If Oscar had not had a hand in the kidnapping, he'd smear gravy on his poncho and eat it for breakfast. The fact that Ellie was abducted so soon after she'd broken the engagement wasn't coincidental. Besides, something smelled fishy when the clerk in the hotel lobby wouldn't let him have side-by-side rooms with Ellie. Evidently the man knew Oscar and gave him Room 202 without even asking or thinking about it. That would explain why no one's name was beside that room number when Colum signed his own name to the register.

Colum had watched as a young boy carried two messages across the street. One to a lady who came immediately to the hotel. Had to be the dressmaker Ellie asked about. The other message went to down the street a little way. Colum figured Oscar would be arriving soon so he carefully set his trap.

To keep awake Colum replayed the scenes of the past days, appreciating Ellie's stamina more and more. Sometime in the middle of the night he dozed, his head resting on his chest, hand resting on the butt of the Colt on his hip. The straight back chair he'd positioned behind the door kept him from truly sleeping. The key easing into his door awoke him with a start, but he sat back in the shadows, hoping the intruder didn't look over his shoulder. If he did, then Colum would be honor bound to just shoot the fellow outright.

Oscar was light on his feet as he tiptoed to the bedside in his stocking feet. He raised the hunting knife high in the air, his silhouette a menacing shadow in the light of the moon drifting through the window. Again and again he brought it down into the pillows Colum had arranged to look like Ellie sleeping with her head beneath the covers.

"I reckon you might have those pillows killed dead by now," Colum finally said, raising to his feet and pointing the Colt right at the man. "Drop the knife, and we'll take a trip across the street to visit with the sheriff."

Oscar lunged at him with the knife, slicing the air as he did and putting himself between Colum and the door. Before Colum could pull back the hammer on the gun, Oscar was in the hallway. "I'll cut you to ribbons," he sneered.

"Put down the knife. It's over," Colum said calmly, pointing the gun between Oscar's wild eyes.

* * *

Ellie arose early, unable to sleep for the nightmares. She'd dressed in her new clothing, wishing Mrs. Whitzel would've brought a pair of new shoes with her. But then she didn't keep shoes in her shop. If Ellie wanted shoes she'd have to go on down the street to have them made. She tugged on her boots and was watching the first faint ribbons of light bringing dawn when she heard the door between her room and Colum's open. Her ears straining to hear what anyone would be doing up so early, she listened intently as someone tiptoed to the next room and opened the door with a key. Well, damn that black-hearted Colum to hell for all eternity. The footsteps were light so it was probably a woman and Colum had visited with her sometime in the night. Most likely when Mrs. Whitzel arrived. That's when it happened. The woman came back to claim her room and Colum "just happened" to peek out the door. He must have given her the key to his room and told her to come visit him any time during the night.

Ellie fumed.

Not that she cared a whit for the dark-haired man. No sir, not one bit. But to think he'd called her all those endearments and then let another woman have the key to his room. Why, he'd even slept with her in the livery stable. Yes, he'd been a gentleman but that didn't matter right now. How could he do such a thing?

She paced the floor, then heard the deep tone of two men's voices arguing. Still angry, she slung open her door to see what was happening at exactly the same time Oscar Wright jumped out into the hallway from Colum's room. When he saw her, he reached out, grabbed a handful of loose blond hair and drug her close to his chest.

"I'll kill her if you don't put that gun down right now," he declared, holding the sharpened edge of the knife to Ellie's delicate throat.

"What is going on? Oscar, are you crazy?" Ellie shouted when she found her voice. All the color had drained from her face, leaving it blanched whiter than St. Peter's robes, and her eyes were wide with pure fear. But only Colum could see that. Oscar only heard a voice full of anger and tried to hang onto a handful of squirming woman.

"Shut up or you are dead. Why didn't you die in that cabin?" Oscar pulled her along backwards with him toward the stairs.

"You knew about that?" Ellie asked through clenched teeth.

"Sure, I did darlin'. Turley and Alvie wouldn't be smart enough to pull off kidnapping fleas off a hound dog. I got a little of that money anyway, didn't I?" Oscar yanked her hair again.

Ellie saw stars in her rage and battled the urge to faint dead away at his feet. She wasn't letting the man take her hostage even if she was lying graveyard dead, her throat slit and bleeding on the hotel carpet. She wiggled and finally in a last ditch effort, stomped down on the place where she figured his boot tip was, connecting the sole of her walking boot to the bones in two of his middle toes. He let go with a scream but didn't even pause as he slid like a kid down the banister to the lobby and ran out the front door. Colum stopped long enough to make sure there was no blood on Ellie's neck, took the steps two at a time and was out the front door, looking both ways in a matter of seconds.

All was as quiet as falling snow. He checked the ground. Footprints from town-folks coming from church went every which way. He eased out farther out onto the sidewalk and listened intently for fast breathing. Nothing. At least not for a full five minutes then three horses came barreling out from between two houses, their riders keeping their heads low as they whizzed past Colum. He aimed his Colt toward the one in the middle but he didn't pull the trigger. He could easily kill the wrong man, one who'd just gotten caught in the wrong bedroom at the wrong time. Just because three men were riding out of town didn't mean any of them were Oscar.

"Where is he?" Ellie stomped out the door, color flooding her pale cheeks and hair tumbling down her back. "Is that them leaving town? Well, stand back and let me at least get off the two shots I've got in this little gun," she said, pointing the derringer at the horses.

"Ain't no use. They're too far away now," he said. "Can't be sure who is who or if either of them is Oscar. Could just be three young boys high tailin' it out of town after church services. Let's go on over to the sheriff's and talk to him since you're already awake."

"Been awake for more than an hour. Why didn't you tell me what you were doing when you switched rooms with me?" She bowed up to him. "I saw what he did to those pillows. It could have been me and you would have been swinging from a rope for doing it, you know? He would have said you did it. You knew he was with them all this time didn't you?"

"Probably, but now he can't, can he? And no, I didn't know all this time. Something wasn't right but I couldn't put my finger on it. I don't know any of those men, but when the stage man told how stupid Turley and Alvie were, it came to me that neither of them could have written that ransom note," Colum said.

"So now I owe you my life again. I'm not so sure I like that," she said, her nose barely six inches from his, color beginning to come back in her cheeks, her shoulders still trembling with a combination of anger and fear.

"You like breathing and not layin' there in the bed with knife wounds all over your pretty body, don't you?" he asked, wishing he could wrap his arms around her and smother her pretty face with passionate kisses. She needed consoling not another round of arguing. Now when did that happen? One minute he could slap her silly for being such an uppity smart aleck. The next he wanted to kiss her? Taste her lips? See how she fit into his arms?

"Oh, hush," she backed down from the fight, glad that the semi-darkness covered the high color filling her cheeks. "Let's go tell the sheriff to put out a poster on Oscar Wright. I'm even putting up a reward. But I don't want him dead or alive. I want to take care of that first part myself." She marched down the sidewalk, her boots sending the loose snow up in clouds as she stomped. "Should've listened to Douglass all along and the two of us should have shot him and buried him in the horse manure beside the barn," she kept a running monologue while Colum had to hustle to keep up with her. "God wouldn't have even taken a stone out of my crown for doing it, either. Did you see how many times he stabbed that pillow? I suppose I'll have to pay for those pillows and the bedding. And by the way, I want that clerk's head on a silver platter, delivered up to me by noon. He told Oscar where I was. I know he did. He sent a note at the same time he sent mine to the dressmaker. I should've figured it out like you did. You knew that abominable, wretched, sorry fool would try to kill me. That's why you switched rooms. I'm going to shoot him right between his eyes and enjoy doing it."

"Whew," Colum let the air out of his lungs in a whoosh. "You are riled."

"That's the first intelligent thing you've said in days," she said, traipsing into the sheriff's office and waking him from a dead sleep.

When she slammed the jailhouse door, making the windows shutter, he came to life, though, sputtering and spitting, trying to wake up. "What the devil? What are you doing here at this time of morning, Miss Hamilton?" He tried to wake up and get his bearings all at the same time.

"Oscar Wright just tried to kill me," she said curtly.

"And who are you?" the sheriff nodded toward Colum.

"He's my bodyguard and the one the family sent to rescue me. His name is Colum Sullivan and that doesn't have a blasted thing to do with what I just said," she told the sheriff. "What are you going to do about this?"

"Well, first thing is I guess you better pull up a chair, Miss Hamilton and commence to telling me just what Oscar Wright has done, then we'll go over to the boarding house and get his story." The sheriff grinned.

"You won't find him there. He and his two sidekicks have left town. The two that kidnapped me. You'll find his boots in Room 202 over at the hotel, though, and while you're checking out my story, you can arrest that clerk. He's an accomplice to the crime," Ellie sat down in the chair, keeping her back ramrod straight and her chin held high.

"Now don't be slinging around accusations," the sheriff said with another condescending grin.

Ellie leaned forward and stared him right in the eyes, her voice low and leaving no room for argument. "Don't you talk down to me, Elias. You see these bruises on my face. Well, there's a good many more on the rest of my body. Those wicked men put them there and left me to die of exposure to the elements. And Oscar was in on the deal. I broke our engagement and he was the ring leader of the kidnapping. He just admitted it to me. I intend that justice is done. So are you going to take care of this? Because if you aren't, I will."

Chapter Eight

Colum drove the rig slowly. Not that he would have had any other option. Unmelted ice and snow kept him from letting the two horses trot along at a comfortable speed. That and an unnerving wariness. Three miles of mountainous road where Oscar could be hiding around every bend, behind every rock or tree. Sunrays played chase through the dead limbs, startling Colum more than once as a trick of light created an illusive figure in the deep shadows of the dormant trees.

"Tell me a story before I lose my mind. I can't believe I was such a sorry judge of character. I was so naive that I figured Oscar would just go away and it was over. Who'd have ever thought he would be in with Turley and Alvie? Would have left me to die in that cabin like that? Now he'll want me dead even worse because there's a price on his head. He can't go back to Shirleysburg. He could be waiting to ambush us as we go home. I've got a case of jitters. Every time something moves I think he's going to jump out and grab me again," she said, barely above a whisper.

"You got that little gun I gave you beneath that cloak?" Colum asked.

"I do and I'd use it, too, in a heartbeat," she nodded.

91

"And you want a story?" Colum asked. "Well, before I tell you a fine old Irish tale, tell me why in the world did you open that hotel door? It wasn't real smart, you know."

"First I heard the door open and someone tiptoeing to your room. Then I heard you two shouting, and I was afraid you . . ." she'd talked herself into a corner. To say that she was worried about him would be admitting right in his presence that she cared what happened to him. To tell him the truth about her jealousy over a fictitious woman who had the key to his room, well, she'd use the gun on herself before she did that.

"You were afraid of what?"

"That you might need my help," she said lamely.

"I see. In that case, I'll thank you but you should have stayed put and I'd have shot the man. It would have been self-defense. He was trying to cut me with that knife. Now he's on the loose and we have to worry about your pretty skin," he said.

Ellie bit her lip to keep from smiling. So she'd been chastised, but she'd also been complimented. He'd said she had pretty skin and he'd said it without one of those sarcastic little endearments. "A story now?" she asked.

"Okay, an Irish one?" he asked.

"That's fine. I don't care if it's Cinderella straight from the book, or even a boy story about pirates and fighting. Anything to keep me from jumping every single time a bird chirps or the sun flickers through the bare tree limbs," she said.

Colum nodded, noticed the bare, drooping limbs of a weeping willow, and a story came to him. So it wasn't Irish. So he was making it up as he drove. Ellie would know neither. "This is the tale of a poor Irish potato farmer who had a dozen sons. The youngest son, Patrick, had no inheritance of course, but he had a good heart and worked hard. On the next farm lived a lovely lass, Colleen, with hair as fair as yours only not as long. Her eyes were as blue as the summer sky, somewhat like yours, too. She was spoiled and pampered as she was the only daughter of a very rich farmer. He had older sons but only one daughter. One day she was walking along the seaside for it wasn't far from their farms and there was Patrick just coming in from a long day of fishing. Now Colleen had never seen the O'Connor sons. Not a one of them because her father kept her very close by his side, so she had no idea that the man was the youngest son of a potato farmer, or that he'd grown up on the farm next to her father's. 'Twas a rare thing that she'd been allowed to walk on the beach alone that day but her chaperone had taken sick at the last minute and she'd not asked her father for permission to go alone. She'd just grabbed her cloak and went, not even thinking that there could be danger in her decision.

"So," Colum cleared his throat and thought about more of the story. *It could be Irish,* he argued with himself. So far it had the makings of a good Irish story. "So Patrick and Colleen met there on the beach with the high cliffs behind them and the gently rolling waves rushing in from the ocean to lap at their feet. They talked for more than an hour and Colleen agreed to meet him right there the next day to talk again. So began the meeting of two hearts."

"It sounds like a pretty story," Ellie said, the deep tone of his voice stilling the tumult in her own breast.

"Ah, but it is a pretty story until now," Colum said. "But Irish stories don't stay pretty too long. They're not for the fainthearted."

"Oh, no, she's not going to die is she?" Ellie asked.

"Not right now. Several months later the winter came and Colleen was so much in love with Patrick that she didn't even notice his threadbare coat or that the pretty trinkets he brought her were seashells or a shock of sea oats. She thought him sentimental and not at all like the young swains who came calling at the mansion bringing her flowers and other more expensive presents. The ones who her father kept parading in front of her. You know the type. The rich ones looking for a wife to set on the shelf and show off when company came 'round.

"Patrick had never been to the mansion so he didn't know who Colleen was. He'd pondered it but finally convinced himself she was a governess to the children who lived in the big house. Then one fine day his father came home from the pub and told him that the wealthy man on the next farm over was hiring help. He was going to expand his house during the slow months of the winter and Patrick, being handy with a hammer, might find work there. Patrick wasted no time in getting his Irish self over to apply for the job, and he was hired on the spot.

"Now, who do you suppose was the first person he saw when the rich man took him inside to show him where he wanted to make the ballroom bigger?" Colum asked.

"Colleen?" Ellie whispered, enthralled with the tale.

"That's right. Colleen, in her fine clothing, sitting on a brocaded settee, having tea from a china cup while three young men vied for her attention. She looked up, unable to believe that her Patrick was just a common laborer. He looked down, unable to believe his Colleen was the daughter of the richest man in County Cork."

Colum waited, collecting his thoughts for the next part.

"Well, go on," Ellie said.

"Patrick worked and worked. Slept in the hay mow above the stables and come the next Sunday, when they always met at the seashore, he slipped away. Whether she was the daughter of his boss or not, he'd fallen in love with her, and it had nothing to do with money. Colleen did the same. She went sneaking out the back door, just like always. Only it wasn't to tell Patrick that she loved him. No, sir. It was to see him one last time and tell him that she couldn't see him again. She'd made inquiries that week, finding out that Patrick was the last son in a long line of O'Connors. The poorest family in all of County Cork.

"Patrick waited under a willow tree back away from the

angry seas that day. Waves more than three feet tall slapped against the beach. Cliffs that had once been so romantic were cold and distant in the afternoon foggy mist. He'd begun to wonder if Colleen would even come out of her warm house now that she knew who he was, but just before their time together would have been up, she appeared. Patrick took that as a good sign and hoped the fairies were looking on with good luck dust on their wings. For today he was going to tell Colleen the desires of his heart and how much he loved her.

"She sat down beside him, keeping her distance. Most usually she kissed him passionately upon arriving. Then she asked him why he hadn't been truthful with her and told her that he was one of the O'Connors? He told her that he hadn't known who she was either and that he loved her deeply from the bottom of his heart. When he'd worked long enough to buy passage to America for the two of them, he wanted her to go with him and they'd start a new life where no one knew he was a ragtag O'Connor or that she was a rich girl."

Ellie was so caught up in the story that she forgot to jump when the naked tree limbs blew in the cold breeze. She forgot about Oscar Wright and the possibility that he could be lying in ambush waiting to shoot Colum or her. She even forgot about the poor, pitiful sympathy everyone would drown her in while surmising behind her back as to what had really happened in that cabin. Ellie wasn't so young and naive as to think they'd believe the truth and nothing but the truth without embellishing it with raised eyebrows and "tut-tuts" behind the palms of their hands. Her solid gold reputation now lay in tatters around her feet, but that didn't matter so much right then as she waited for Colum to finish his fairytale.

"Colleen threw back her pretty head and laughed at Patrick. Of course, she'd been infatuated with him. Of course, they'd shared a few kisses, but that didn't mean she had fallen in love with him, or that she'd get on a ship and go across the ocean to America and start anew. Why should she? She already had everything in the world. Money, suitors by the dozens, jewels, parties, a father who doted on her, a mother who thought the sun only came up in the morning to shine on Colleen's golden hair. No, she would not entertain such a silly notion. And if Patrick told one person that they had been meeting without a chaperone, then she would have him fired and her father would most likely ask him out to a duel."

Ellie's heart stopped. She'd been so sure that Colleen would show more spirit. That she'd throw caution right out into the big waves and tell Patrick they could run away together right then. "So what happened? Is that the end of the tale? Mary, mother of Christ, do Irish tales always end so terribly?"

"No, it's not the end of the tale, *querida,*" Colum said with a smile. But he knew where the end was going now. Had it worked out in his mind.

"Colleen went home, and Patrick went back to work. Every day he saw her, flirting with the young men, wallowing in the lap of luxury. His heart broke anew every day but he kept working. For a whole year he worked until he had enough money for passage to America. Standing on the ship, watching his mother weep and his father wave, he still hoped he would see Colleen there with a bag and a changed mind. Even then he would have gone back to her father's house to work another year for the money for her passage if she would have given him an ounce of encouragement. But she didn't appear on that bright sunny day. He couldn't even blame a misty fog and pretend she'd been there and he couldn't see her.

"So Patrick came to America and started anew. He worked as a carpenter for a big firm, saved his money and bought his own business. Before many years went by, he was a rich man. Women flocked around him, seeing a handsome man with his own business. But Patrick couldn't see past his precious Irish Colleen to give them the time of day. He grew to be a very old rich man and died, leaving all his amassed fortune to his brother's sons across the sea. At his request they carried his body back to Ireland and buried him there on the cliffs overlooking the beach where he and Colleen had met so many times. Also fulfilling his wishes, they planted a willow tree at the head of his tombstone, and the next spring after he'd died, when the new leaves came on the tree, the limbs drooped to the ground, crying for the love that could not be. And that's the story of the weeping willow."

Ellie sat very still, wonder filling her breast at such love. To be loved so much that even when the love was tossed back in your face, that it did not die. Unconditional love. Complete absolution. Utter forgiving. No strings. Just pure sweet love that saw past the hurt of the rejection and kept on loving.

"And Colleen?" she asked.

"A year passed from the time she met Patrick at the willow tree for the last time. Then one day Patrick didn't come to work so she asked her father about the carpenter who still had some work to do on the ballroom. Her father told her that the O'Connor lad had taken his savings and was sailing that very day to America. What a silly boy he was, according to her father. But then the O'Connors weren't known for their brains, just their ability to produce sons. She arrived at the dock in time to see the ship on the far horizon, and wept bitterly. Too late she'd found that she loved Patrick O'Connor and that none of the other young suitors would do. She drug her heavy heart back to the mansion but was unable to find peace there. So she went for a lonely walk to the beach, to the willow tree where she'd spurned his love. There she found a letter, saying that he would always hold her in the depths of his heart whether she loved him or not and that all he had to do was close his eyes to see her beauty and sweet smile. He'd placed a lovely seashell on it to hold it down. She never married and became known in

County Cork for her strange ways. Every day she walked to the beach, a bag in her hand with nothing in it but the seashell and letter and she waited for an hour, searching the horizon for a ship bringing her Patrick back to her. She grew old and one day the ship did come. It brought her sweet Patrick back, only he was in a wooden box and they buried him high on the cliffs overlooking their private spot. The next week she died and at her request and the amazement of everyone in County Cork, was buried beside him under the weeping willow."

"How sad," Ellie said. "How utterly sad. Do all Irish stories make a person want to weep?"

"Most of them. Life is like that Miss Hamilton. You grab it by the horns, look it right in the eye and dare it to challenge you. Or else you live with your rash decision and look back and wish you'd done things differently. The heart is a strange thing. It can't see. It can't hear. It can only feel and the wisdom it has in that is beyond our knowledge," Colum said.

"Quite the philosopher, aren't you?" Ellie said. "Couldn't you have told the story differently? Maybe made the fairies grab their souls and take them away to a land where they could be together forever in the afterlife."

"Perhaps they are, *querida*," he said. "But that is not for us to know. Only the two old people buried on that cliff with a weeping willow tree crying tears for what could not be in their lifetime know what happens in the afterlife. Look. We are ready to turn down the lane to the house. You've been rescued and if I can get you a quarter of a mile farther, you'll be home."

Suddenly, Ellie's hands were clammy. Home. She'd left her room on that horrible night a naive young woman. One who'd seen the horrors of war, but had not known the cruelty a man can do to a woman. One who'd trusted a man with her whole heart, soul, and life only to find that she'd been terribly wrong. She'd found another Elspeth Joy Hamilton in the past days. Colum had helped her to find that person and even though she wanted to be home, she didn't want Colum to leave. And leave he would. To go back to his precious Texas where there was very little snow and lots of hot summer days.

A part of her could hardly wait to get home, amongst her things and her family. The other part lay in a confused jumble, much like Colleen must have felt that day when she got to the dock just in time to see her heart going to America. How did a woman live without a heart, with only the shell of a body where it had once been? *She went crazy, that's what she did,* Ellie thought as Colum eased the rig down the lane toward the house. Smoke spiraled up from the chimneys. Was that Monroe coming in from the barn? There went Douglass out to greet him, kissing him passionately on the mouth right out there for everyone to see. Ellie would never have a love like that. Not in her position. No man would ever want her, and she wasn't sure she wanted a man in her life. But if she did, it would be someone to make her laugh, to make her fighting mad, to stir her emotions like Colum Sullivan did. And she could not allow herself to even like that man . . . much less love him. Ellie needed lots of time to get things in order, to figure out what was happening, and she was afraid she didn't have it.

Chapter Nine

They gathered around the dining room table, a platter of cookies, a pot of coffee and one of tea, in the middle. Douglass and Monroe sat close together on one side, Indigo and Ellie on the other, Laura at one end and Colum at the other. Between Ellie and Colum the story had been told. Tears dripped from Laura's cheeks onto the white collar of her wool dress. To think that her sweet niece had been put through such an ordeal was more burden than her heart could bear. If Oscar Wright had a brain in his head, he'd be putting enough distance between him and Laura Hamilton that he never showed his face in that part of Pennsylvania again. Because if Laura found him lurking around Love's Valley, he was a dead man. Plain and simple.

"Don't cry, Aunt Laura," Ellie patted her hand. "I'm alive and the bruises will heal. It could have been much, much worse. I forgot to tell you the tinker came by right after Colum unshackled me and Colum bought a whole case of snake oil. You know nothing could stand up against that vile stuff. And he made me take two big spoonfuls three times a day."

"Good for him," Laura wiped the tears away. There was a

100

new strength in Ellie's voice and demeanor, but the cost at which it came was almighty dear.

Good for him in lots of ways, Ellie thought. *Good for him for rescuing me, for telling me about the fairies on that long trek out of Blacklog Valley, for carrying me into the church, for sleeping with me and not molesting me, for figuring out that Oscar was at the root of the kidnapping, for switching room keys with me to keep Oscar from plunging that knife into my body like he did the pillows. Good for him because he'll be leaving tomorrow most likely and I can work on getting myself put back together.*

"We got your letter a couple of days ago. Now we know what you meant by being able to travel. We also had a telegram from Flannon yesterday," Douglass reached to take Colum's hand in hers. "He's stuck in southern Virginia for a few days until the snow melts and the stage can go on. Monroe tells me it was a short autumn season even for this area and winter is here to stay, Colum. I'm going to beg now, Colum, so get ready for it."

Colum rolled his brown eyes and grinned. He had the softest heart of all six Sullivan brothers when it came to Douglass. She could bend him around her smallest finger with a few tears. "Beg all you want, my little sister, but if it's got one thing to do with going out in that bitter wind to rescue another stray person, the answer is no."

"Stray person?" Ellie's eyes blazed across the table. "Is that what I am to you? Just a stray person? Someone you rescued to keep your sister happy?"

Douglass was taken aback for a moment, then she smiled. So that was the way of it. She wondered if either of them knew yet. Colum was more stubborn than an rangy old Longhorn steer at spring round-up. That was the Sullivan-Montoya bloodlines and it couldn't be helped. It looked like the same rang true for the Hamilton bloodline because Ellie was about to jump over the table and slap Colum into next week and enjoy doing it. Douglass loved it, absolutely loved it. If they'd wake up and listen to their hearts, they'd realize that they had a lot in common. Oh, to think about Colum staying in Love's Valley. Douglass slid her hand away from Colum's and held both of hers tightly in her lap to keep from clapping and jumping up to dance a jig around the table.

"Of course you are a stray, Miss Hamilton," Colum said curtly. "Did you think after you marred my face for the rest of my life with those deadly fingernails of yours, I would have rushed right out and rescued you without some begging and pleading? It even took tears and threats if you must know the full extent of Douglass's love for you."

"You're no better than . . ." she stopped before she said the name, *Oscar*. That wasn't true and she'd just be saying it to shove an arrow deep into his heart. He was better than that contemptible excuse for a man.

"Than what? Than who?" Colum glared at her, the two of them suddenly the only people in the dining room. The space between them crackled and snapped with raw emotions, begging to be let loose to explore the possibility of love.

"Than a sorry Rebel skunk," Ellie snapped at him.

"That's the truth," Indigo jumped into the foray. "He's just a Rebel and don't you forget it, Ellie. Just like those that burned your house and killed your parents."

"You hush," Ellie turned on her. "This isn't your fight. It's mine. And don't you be putting in your opinions. I know what he is and who he is, and if I want to call him names that's fine, but you better not say a word, Indigo Hamilton."

"Well, I do declare," Indigo puffed up. Lord have mercy and saint's alive, but Ellie had done gone and fallen for a rebel. Indigo wouldn't have believed it of her in a million years. It must have something to do with the fact that Oscar had proven to be such a low down creature and Colum had gone to her rescue when she thought she was going to die. Well, Indigo could take care of the problem in no time at all.

She'd bring Ellie to her senses if she had to use severe force. The fact that Monroe came dragging in a southern Rebel who was half-Mexican and half-Irish was more than Indigo could handle. She'd fight tooth, nail, hair, and eyeball to keep another Rebel from setting up squatter's rights in Love's Valley.

"Children, children," Laura chuckled. Seemed like maybe Ellie had some feelings for her rescuer. Laura didn't mind. She wasn't one of those women who held grudges. The war had been fought and it was over now. Life went on, and if Ellie found herself in love with Colum, well, so be it. Laura had had her own share of problems when Harrison Milford Hamilton first brought her to Love's Valley. She'd been outspoken at a time when women for sure kept their mouth shut and listened to their husbands, and she'd come from a poor, poor family in Shade Valley. Harrison's mother about had an apoplexy right there in the living room when he introduced Laura as his wife. Laura had vowed it didn't matter who her children married, so long as there was love in the marriage. And she'd stand by that vow, no matter what.

"You don't have to fight my battles," Colum said. "I'm perfectly capable of taking care of myself, even with a snotnosed little smart mouth like Indigo."

"Well, you just made it my battle by calling me those names," Indigo shot daggers across the table at Colum. "I'm not a snot-nosed little smart mouth."

"Prove it," Colum said, hiding a grin. He'd argued with Douglass all her life and she was a master of disputing. Indigo was barely a novice compared to his sister.

"I don't have to prove anything to the likes of you," Indigo said, sliding back her chair and leaving the room with her nose high and her feathers most definitely ruffled.

"You were saying something about begging?" Ellie turned to Douglass. "Seems like before we started this row that you said something about begging Colum?"

"I sure did." A smile split Douglass's dainty features and

her crystal clear blue eyes danced with merriment. "I'm going to beg until Colum says yes. You see, Monroe and I have got the plans all done for our new house which is going to be just down the Valley a bit. A big old two-story white house with pillars on the front porch and two chimneys. Monroe says we can start it right away and we can hire the laborers from town to come out here and stay in the bunkhouse out back. But we need a master carpenter to oversee the whole job. Monroe can help with the building in between all the other things he's got to do here on the farm until the other two brothers come home, but the problem is he can't oversee the work every day. That's where the begging comes in, Colum. Would you please stay the winter with us and help build our new home? It would mean so much more if you had a hand in it."

Now that's just what he did not want to do, with lots of emphasis on the word, *not!* Stay in Love's Valley and build a house with Ellie right under his feet, and worse yet, Indigo with her hatred of anything that ever took a breath south of the Mason-Dixon line. He rubbed his chin and let his fingers go to the scar on his face. He'd figured he'd have to stay put for a while anyway since winter had come early, but he might as well make Douglass beg a bit before he gave in.

"The only thing that kept me going on that walk out of that forsaken Blacklog Valley place was the sight of Texas in my vision," he said.

"I'll pay whatever you want," Monroe said.

"Family don't take money from its own for things like that," Colum said, winking at Monroe from behind his hand. "Wouldn't think of charging you. Just don't know if I can stand to live in the same house with all these sharp-tongued women. Back in Texas, there was Granny, but she lived down the road. Momma can slice ribbons with her tongue when she's upset, but us boys learned early on to stay out of her way when she was showing her Mexican temper. Then we had Douglass who whined around . . ."

"I never whined," she slapped his arm. "Not one time. If I'd whined you six, big mean boys wouldn't have ever let me hear the end of it. Don't you go tellin' my handsome new husband I whined."

Colum chuckled. "Of course I'll stay and oversee the building of your new house. If, and only if, Monroe will protect me from you women."

"I'll do you one better. You can stay out in the bunkhouse and not even have to look at these women. The men will live there until the work is done. Those who are married will most likely go home a night or two a week and on Saturday night to stay over until Sunday night. Only time you'll have to even look at these Hamilton women is when you take your meals and then you can ignore them. Is that agreeable?" Monroe asked.

Ellie's heart stopped beating, then took off with a full head of steam so fast she thought the buttons would pop right off her new shirt waist. Colum was staying at the ranch until spring anyway, only a stone's throw away and she'd see him often even if it was only at meal time. She'd prepared herself for good-byes and now he was going to be underfoot for six months. Maybe it was for the best. Maybe a higher power had intervened to show her that Colum was after all just a man like all the rest. At least, he wouldn't leave like Patrick did in the story, with her heart still tied up in knots over the way she felt toward him. No, sir. She had a full six months to get over the man, and she could sure enough depend on Indigo to help her with the task at hand. With the two of them working on it, night and day, it shouldn't take more than a week or two to cleanse her heart of the crazy, mixed-up feelings she had every time she looked at Colum Sullivan.

"I've hired ten good men from town and they'll be here tomorrow morning," Monroe said. "Let's take our coffee to the parlor and I'll show you the plans Douglass and I've come up with," he bent down to kiss his pretty wife's lips before they left. He'd never get enough of kissing and loving Douglass Esmerelda. Looking back, he believed from the depths of his heart that God himself had planted her in the middle of the road especially for him on that hot Texas fall day.

"I'll go up with Ellie to her room and get her tucked in for a rest," Douglass said.

"I'm not going anywhere for a rest," Ellie said. "There's work a plenty to be done around here and I'm helping. I didn't escape death to be molly coddled. Now what's on the menu for lunch? And since this is Tuesday, I believe there's probably ironing stacked knee deep in the kitchen so get the irons out and let's get them heated."

"Yes, ma'am," Douglass giggled. "Does that snake oil you talked about change everyone this much?"

"No, but Turley and Alvie, not to mention that lowdown snake, Oscar, could change a house kitten into a mountain lion," Ellie snorted. "By the way, you sure look happy, Douglass."

"I am, Ellie. Never been happier. Even with this bitter cold winter coming so soon, my heart is full," she said.

"That's good," Ellie said. "Aunt Laura, let's make fried chicken for dinner. I'm so sick of rabbit stew, I could die. And mashed potatoes with real butter, and gravy with real cream," she started toward the kitchen, rolling up her sleeves.

"I believe that girl has faced death and come out with a whole new attitude," Laura picked up the coffee pot and followed her.

Douglass grabbed the tea pot and brought up the rear of the parade. "Does that to a woman, sometimes," she said. "Ellie, how about biscuits and a jar of green beans?"

"Sounds good to me. I'll peel potatoes if you'll talk Indigo into killing a couple of chickens and plucking them," she tossed over her shoulder just as Indigo came through the door.

"I'd love to. The way I feel right now, I need to murder something. Might as well be a couple of chickens, but the truth be known, I'd rather kill that rebel in there who's been invited to stay around until spring," she said.

"Be careful," Douglass narrowed her eyes at her sister-in-law. "That's my brother you'd be talkin' about. You wouldn't want me to talk about your brother like that."

"No, I would not. But Monroe is perfect and yours is a rebel," Indigo said, grabbing her jacket from a peg beside the door and storming outside into the cold.

Colum spent the whole day going over the plans for the new house, worrying through the list of supplies the sawmill had already delivered and making another list of what was lacking. He ate a scrumptious dinner with the family with Ellie across the table. Once their hands brushed as she passed him a platter piled high with crispy fried chicken and sparks flew, but Colum didn't have time to analyze them. He, Douglass, and Monroe were talking about how many white pillars they'd use on the front porch. At supper, the same thing happened. Ellie passed the butter across the table and there was the jolt again, but still he ignored it.

However, when he unrolled the mattress at the far end of the bunkhouse, he couldn't ignore the feelings any longer. He tucked the flannel sheet under the sides of the mattress, made crisp military corners and flipped the top blanket over that, all the while trying to escape thinking about Elspeth Hamilton. He did all the things a man has to do before he goes to bed, forcing himself to keep his mind on washing up, the work lined up for the next day, combing his unruly black hair, blowing out the flame in the lamp, anything but Ellie.

He slipped between the covers on the bed, laid his tired head back on the pillow, and the visions came to visit in the darkness. *So I like the woman,* he thought. That wasn't anything to worry about. He'd liked Clara O'Toole last year, and after a few dances and picnics had found he didn't like her anymore. Colum was twenty-eight years old. He'd spent the whole war fighting and tracking. He'd liked lots of women but he'd never loved a woman. And love Elspeth Hamilton, he most certainly did not. When he fell in love it was going to be with a short, dark-haired, dark-eyed girl from Bowie County, Texas, preferably from right in DeKalb. The girl of his dreams would be quiet, submissive, an excellent cook and would dote on him. She'd never raise a fuss like Ellie did at the table that morning, and she most assuredly wouldn't scratch his face in a fight because she wouldn't fight with Colum. Whatever he said, she would obey.

"So there," he said, the matter decided. It wasn't so unusual to have feelings for Ellie for a few days. After all, he'd have feelings for a kitten he'd rescued from a dog. He'd pet it for a few days but soon the kitten would go on about its business and Colum would go about his. That's what was happening right now. Finally, the job was finished. Now Colum would begin a new one and in a few days he'd have Ellie put in the same category as Indigo. Sassy. Yankee. Definitely not for him.

Ellie pulled back the drapes in her bedroom, drew her shawl tightly around her shoulders as she listened to the cold wind howling down the valley. Stars glittered in the dark skies and clouds drifted in and out across the white moon. A faint light flickered through the window at the far end of the bunkhouse. What was he thinking about as he got ready for bed?

"Most likely about his sister's house," Ellie told herself. She dropped the drapes when the yellow light in the window was extinguished and crawled into her own bed. She wiggled her way down into the feathers and sighed. Luxury. Pure luxury that no one could take from her again.

She rolled onto her side and tucked her hands under her cheek. Yes, Colum was handsome beyond words. Yes, he had been a gentleman of impeccable quality. Yes, he'd kept her entertained with his stories. All those things drew her to him, but now they were back in the real world, where there were no Patrick O'Connors nor were there Colleens. In the real world, there was Elspeth Joy Hamilton who'd just endured a frightening experience and came out on the other side still a whole woman, mind intact. A woman of English descent, who had no use for a southern man. On the other side was Colum, not only southern, but Irish and Mexican, doubling the bad qualities. There was actually nothing to get over. She'd merely had a reaction to his touch because he'd come to her rescue. In a week, neither of them would be able to stay in the same room together without a major outbreak.

She shut her eyes and dreamed of sitting beneath a willow tree in the spring of the year. Colum begged her to go to a foreign country called Texas and she refused. She couldn't leave her blessed Love's Valley and live amongst the monsters who'd ruined her world with a fire. She awoke in the middle of the night, her pillow wet with tears and her heart in a tangled knot. Such a silly dream. It would never happen anyway. She'd only dreamed it because of that story he told. She pulled the covers tight around her neck and went back to sleep only to pick up the dream at the exact place she'd left it when she awoke. She was an old woman, sitting beside her parents' graves and weeping for a love that she'd thrown away.

At daybreak, three men watched two wagon loads of workers arrive at the Hamilton house. The three were hidden deep back in the trees, huddled down in their coats, guns drawn and ready.

"We could have stormed the house and killed them all but now there's too many of them. Why'd we have to sit here and let all that help come in anyway?" Turley said.

"I ain't got no beef with Monroe that I'd want to kill him. He did pay us half of the money we asked for, didn't he?" Oscar grinned. "It's that woman who's ruined my life. She was supposed to die in that cabin. Then she was supposed to die when I stabbed her, only it was pillows. She must be half cat. But two of her lives are gone now and my turn will come. Someday I'll get my turn at her again and when I do there won't be any leaving her to the wolves and bears. I'll make her wish she'd never scorned me. Then I'll make her wish she'd never put a price on my head. She's the one that's turned me into an outlaw. But even outlaws have got to live. So let's go to Chambersburg and rob a bank."

"Now that's talking sense," Alvie spit a long string of tobacco juice onto the white snow. "This waiting around for rich women don't put money in our pockets right now. And that money Monroe give us ain't going to keep us long."

"Way you gambled away your part at poker over in Shade Gap, it would take a fortune to keep you supplied," Oscar snapped at him.

"Who cares. There's lots of money in the banks, ain't there? More than what you get from knockin' some old maid on the back of the head and tying her up, anyway," Alvie laughed.

"We'll sit right here and wait for those men to go about their business then we'll ride out of this place. We'll come back though and that's a promise. And when we do, Ellie Hamilton, you are a dead woman. I'll teach you to throw me over. I woulda made you a decent husband," Oscar talked out loud but not to Alvie or Turley.

"Sure you would have. At least she would have thought you were makin' a decent husband," Turley laughed. "Just like them other four women did. Right up until you walked away with all their money."

Oscar grinned. "Settle in for a little bit, boys. Looks like that Rebel and Monroe are going to give a talk to those men. Can't ride out without being seen right now. Wonder what in the devil is going on there anyway? They wouldn't have called in that much help to hunt us down. Monroe wouldn't pay out that kind of money, not even for his kin. Leastwise, I don't think he would. Man might be crazier than I figured."

Chapter Ten

"Good morning," Monroe greeted the men in the bunk-house yard. A tall man with striking black hair and deep brown eyes, he turned most women's heads when he walked by. But he was also a man's man, a captain in the Union army, one of the select few the President of the United States had sent to Texas to oversee the reconstruction after the war. In his own part of the country, Love's Valley, Pennsylvania, he was respected because he'd earned the respect as Monroe Hamilton, not just because he was Harrison Hamilton's son.

A mumbled round of greetings met him. "I want to intro-duce you to my brother-in-law, Colum Sullivan, from Texas, who is going to be the chief overseer on this job. There'll be three squares a day, plenty of good food. Work will begin as soon as it's light enough to see and quit when it's too dark to see the nails. That's a short day this time of year. I'll trust you've all had breakfast this morning and are eager to get at it. Colum has the plans for the house laid out on the floor of the bunkhouse and he'll explain what's going on for the next few minutes, then we'll all go to work. Today, I've got noth-ing planned so I'm working with you. As soon as Colum tells me where he wants me," Monroe said.

"Is this here the brother of that southern woman you married?" one of the men from the back asked.

"Yes, it is," Monroe said firmly.

"Then I'm goin' on back home," the man said.

Colum had been leaning on the porch post and nothing had happened so far to surprise him. He stepped up to the edge of the porch and let his eyes roam over the men there. For a few minutes silence prevailed. "Ya'll might want to reconsider your decision to work here for the next few months. I am a Texan. I was a Confederate soldier in the war, but the war is over. I am from the south and I am half-Irish and half-Mexican. I will work along beside you and I'm a fair man. This is not the first house I've helped build. You, there," he pointed to an older man with a crop of pure white hair. "What's your name?"

"I'm Bill Smith," the man said.

"You stayin' or goin'?" Colum asked.

"I reckon I'm stayin'. Ain't no one else will hire an old man like me and I need the work. I don't give a rat's hind end where you come from boy, long as I get my paycheck at the end of the week. Like you said, war's over, and it's time to move on," Bill said.

"Then your first job is to drive one of those wagons back into Shirleysburg and pick up the supplies on this list. While you're going you can haul any of these men back who don't want to work here. Monroe and I expect a full day's work for a full day's pay and without grumbling because the overseer is any of the things I just mentioned. If you've got a gripe with that, then Bill here will take you back to town. Here's that list. Put the things on it on Mr. Monroe's bill and be back here quick as you can. The ones of you who need to work and are staying can follow me and Monroe inside," he said. In Colum's north Texas world he was as respected as Monroe was in Love's Valley. In the Confederate army he'd been as important as Monroe had been in the Union army. But the war was over and it was truly time to move on.

Three men crawled up in the back of the wagon with Bill and shot mean looks at Monroe as they rode away. They'd come to work for a Hamilton, not a Rebel, and the war might be over for the almighty-big-shot Hamiltons, but it wasn't for them. They'd lost relatives and friends and it would never be over.

"These are the plans," Colum pointed toward the paper stretched out on the floor. "Today we work on the first level, the foundation. Without a firm, true, steady foundation you're wasting your time building the rest of the house. I'll be checking every single board as it goes into that foundation and if it's not perfect, then it will come back out and be redone. Monroe and Douglass have decided against a basement under the house. We'll start today by leveling the ground and setting the pilings to hold this big thing up. There's a bite in the air this morning, but the sun is out, so let's go to work. Any questions?"

"Yes, you the one who went out there and brought Miss Ellie back from that kidnapping?" one man asked.

"I am," Colum said.

"Is it right that you carried your saddle the whole way down out of Blacklog Valley?" he asked.

"It is," Colum said.

"Reckon I won't have no trouble with a man who'd do that," he said. "I'm Claude and I've built many a house in these parts. Show me where the new Mrs. Hamilton has a mind to set this big mansion and I'll pass judgment on whether the land will hold her up."

"I'm glad to have you working with us, Claude," Colum said.

Murmurings in the back of the room let him know some of the other men needed the work too bad to go back to town with Bill but they weren't one bit impressed with his rescue skills or his love for his saddle either. That, too, was to be expected. They didn't have to be his best friends. They simply needed to work hard.

"The site is down the valley about a half a mile. There's two wagons out there with everything we need to get started. Load up, men, and we'll be on our way," Monroe was the first one out the door.

Douglass sat side saddle on her favorite horse, right beside the first wagon. This first day she fully well intended to see that her house was put exactly where she wanted it. She didn't care if they had to move hell and half of Texas to make it work. She wanted to see the sun coming up over those mountains every morning and she wanted that particular willow tree to be in her backyard. Sure, she could plant one, but she'd be old and gray before it was that big and she already had a plan for a bench under the branches of the willow tree, a garden all around it with stepping stones among the roses and ferns.

"Good morning, I'm Douglass Hamilton," she greeted the men in the wagons.

"That's not a girl's name," a voice said from the middle of the men in one wagon.

"Nope, it's not," Douglass smiled brightly, winning several hearts with her beauty. "But my father is Irish, you see, and my Momma is Mexican. They decided when the first baby was on the way that he would give them a fine Irish name and she could give them a fine Mexican second name. Six sons later, of which Colum Eduardo, is the second one, I was born," she explained as they rode down the valley toward her home site. "Now Daddy already had the name Douglass picked out for his seventh son. Only to everyone's surprise I was a girl. Momma says he was so speechless that they finally had a daughter after a six pack of worthless Irish-Mexican sons that he couldn't think of a fine Irish girl's name so they kept the name Douglass."

One of the men slapped his thigh. "My wife is about to have her first. If it's a girl I think I'll name her Stanley after me."

"Sounds like a wonderful idea to me," Douglass said.

"Now, you fellers have got to know one thing about this house building. I'll be in your hair some of the time just because that's the way I am and because I'll have to keep Colum on his toes. He's a hard worker and a fair man, an excellent carpenter. But he works better and faster if he's angry and that's my job, to keep him about half mad all the time. And there's a big old willow tree in what is going to be my backyard. I don't want a single limb of it cut back or damaged in any way," she told them.

"Yes, ma'am," Claude said.

Ellie and Indigo watched the parade heading off up the valley from the back porch. Douglass and the first wagon in the lead. Colum, cutting a fine figure driving the second wagon. Ellie could see the folly in letting her silly broken heart look upon Colum with admiration, though. Grease and water didn't mix. Not when they were cold. Especially when they were heated up.

"You're not in love with that worthless rebel, are you?" Indigo asked bluntly, flipping her long hair over her shoulder, her blue eyes shooting enough bullets at the wagons that there would be one dead former confederate soldier if she could kill with mere looks.

"Love?" Ellie almost choked on the spoken word.

"Well, it's written all over you. You look just like Douglass did when she'd look at Monroe and I'm telling you right now, Ellie, it ain't going to happen again. I can barely hold my head up in Shirleysburg as it is. Holy Mother of Christ, if I ever marry it'll be a pure miracle with that kind of tainting on the Hamilton blood," Indigo said.

"Just because you don't like him doesn't mean I can't," Ellie puffed up. "But love him? Holy smoke, girl, Oscar Wright just proved to me how devious a man can be. If you think I'm going to give my heart away again so soon you've got less brains than the whole rebel army of the south."

There, she'd said it. Or had she? She hadn't actually said she didn't love him, just that she wouldn't.

"That's good," Indigo said. "Because if you'd admitted it, I would have done everything in my power to put an end to it. I mean it, Elspeth Joy Hamilton. I won't have another member of my family drag in one of that kind."

"I'd say you don't have a thing to worry about," Ellie mumbled, suddenly cross at her young cousin for being so hateful.

"I've got my eye on Charlie Brewster's younger brother. He's been flirting with me when I go into the general store," Indigo said seriously.

"He's a good man," Ellie said. A sad fellow most of the time but maybe Indigo with her lovely face could make him smile.

"Of course he is. Served his country down in southern Virginia for the whole war. Took a bullet in his left arm and was lucky they didn't have to cut it off," Indigo said. "Now do you want to take a morning walk up there where they're starting the work just so Douglass won't be the only female with all those men?"

"Yes, I would love a morning walk," Ellie said. Not so she could see how Colum operated with men or how he'd look with a hammer in his hands. No, sir, she wasn't going to give in to the fluttery feeling in the pit of her stomach every time she was around the man. Like Indigo said, it was just to give Douglass a bit of support.

Colum was aware of Ellie's presence before he even looked around and saw her talking with his sister, Douglass. Ellie was a picture of beauty, for the world looking like something the devil sugar-coated to cause him to fall into a puddle of pure sin. Turning back to the job at hand, he ignored her. At least physically. The prickle on the back of his neck, the clamminess in his palms, the dryness in his mouth told him he wasn't really fooling anyone but himself. The only thing to do was plunge himself into hard, hard work and forget the woman. In the spring he'd go home to Texas and she'd just be a pleasant memory.

"Well, hello, Miss Indigo," one of the men waved.

Indigo waved back but she didn't smile.

"I'd say Melvin might be interested in you," Ellie whispered.

"I'd say Melvin can forget me," Indigo said. "I've already made my choice and I'm not changing my mind."

"At your age?" Douglass asked, whipping around to look at Indigo in a new light.

"Yes, at my age. I'm not a child. In case you haven't noticed I'm taller than you are and I can run a household. Two of my closest friends have already been married long enough to have a baby," Indigo said.

"I'm just an old maid," Ellie managed a weak smile in her cousin's defense. "And you were on the verge of being one when Monroe found you."

"I sure was. By Texas standards, I probably couldn't have even paid a man to marry me I was so far over the line. Why I was all of twenty years old the week before I got married," Douglass laughed. "But forget that. I'm so excited I could shout. They said the house could easily be built here. You'll both have to help me decide about wallpaper and furniture."

"Pretty free with my brother's money aren't you?" Indigo said, hoping her barb stuck tight in Douglass's heart and stung.

"No, I am not," Douglass set her jaw and glared at her sister-in-law. "His money is building this house. My money is furnishing it. I'm not a poor child from the wrong side of the tracks, Indigo. I'm bringing as much of my own money into this marriage as your brother has."

"Oh, really," Indigo smarted off. "And where did the likes of you get money of your own?"

"It's a long story," Douglass said. "And quite frankly not

a blessed bit of your business, young lady. Just rest assured not one dime of your sweet inheritance is going into my new home."

"Oh, I know it's not," Indigo said. "If it were, I'd raise a fuss that would make the war look like a little boy's game with sticks for rifles."

"Stop it, Indigo," Ellie said. "You know you like Douglass."

"In your dreams," Indigo said. "She's a rebel, a southerner and a stupid Irishman's daughter," Indigo said.

Douglass took two steps forward and looked up into Indigo's eyes. "If you've got a brain in your head you will use it to remember not to slur my father, my mother, my heritage or my birth again. Grow up, Indigo Hamilton. If you are so all fired ready to make a home of your own, get married and have children. You need to grow up and stop being so hateful."

"I could slap you so hard you'd take a week to wake up," Indigo said.

"You might, but then you'd have to face the wrath of this Mexican pouring down upon your head," Douglass said in a tone that left no doubt she meant what she said.

Indigo's blood ran cold. She'd pushed the woman as far as she dared. "I'm going back home now. Are you coming with me?" she asked Ellie, ignoring Douglass.

"No, I'm going to stay a spell and watch them work on the foundation," Ellie said. Let Indigo walk home alone and think about her smart mouth. Maybe it would do her more good than anything.

"So forget about Indigo's temper and tell me about the house," Ellie said as Indigo stormed back up the valley.

"It's two stories, with a full finished attic. Six bedrooms upstairs. We want a big family. Lots of kids," Douglass blushed.

"So is Colum your oldest brother?" Ellie asked out of the clear blue winter sky and then could have easily bitten her tongue off.

"No, he's the second to the oldest. Patrick is the oldest one. Then Colum, Keven, Nicolaus, Brendon, and Flannon. Six of them and then me. Tell me something. Do you have feelings for Colum?" Douglass asked, barely above a whisper.

The blunt question took Ellie completely by surprise. Heat crept up from her neck filling her cheeks with high color. "I don't know, Douglass. I just flat don't know. I think there's a respect there because he came to rescue me and was so kind all the way back home. Could be, I'm just suffering from the effects of what I went through. I really thought I'd die with pneumonia in that cabin. It was so cold and I was so hungry. Then suddenly it was warm and clean and Colum was there helping me get well."

"You've got a few months to figure it out, I suppose. You could surely do a lot worse than my brother, Ellie," Douglass said.

"I suppose so, but your brother couldn't pick a woman with a worse reputation than mine right now, so the problem is solved," Ellie said.

Before Douglass could answer, Monroe left the men who'd started working with shovels, digging in the frozen earth. He slipped his arm around Douglass's waist and drew her tightly to his side. "Before summer if we can keep enough hands out here, we should be living in it. Seems kind of strange thinking about that when there's nothing there right now, doesn't it?"

"Anything is possible with lots of work and a good foundation," Douglass leaned into the embrace, hoping that her words sunk into Ellie's heart and became more than just words.

"So what do you think, little sister?" Colum joined them for a few minutes.

"I think I'm the luckiest woman on earth," she said. "Now if I could just keep you here forever instead of just a few months."

Colum looked at Ellie, who was holding her breath.

"I don't think so. As soon as I've got you settled in this house, I'm going home. Texas is calling my name and I can hardly wait to get back there. And how are you this morning, Miss Hamilton? Glad to be back in your own feather bed, I would suppose?"

"Yes, I am, but gentlemen don't talk about women and their beds," she said.

"Not even when . . ." his eyes glittered.

"Hush!" She admonished, slapping him on the shoulder, her hand suddenly on fire from the mere touch in spite of the crisp wind stirring the bare tree limbs.

"Ah, I think I hear a story here," Douglass giggled. "And while you big strong men fight this cold unyielding earth, I'm going to walk back to the house with Ellie and try to pry it out of her."

"Give me a kiss first," Monroe bent to touch Douglass's lips with his own. "The honeymoon isn't over yet, is it?"

"Never. Not even close," she wrapped her arms around her husband's neck and really kissed him, not caring that the men were watching or that it embarrassed the very devil out of both Colum and Ellie.

"Colum, you are blushing," Douglass teased.

"Monroe can't you control this woman you married?" he said hoarsely, hoping his attempt at humor covered the fact he was indeed crimson as a pickled beet.

"Nope, got a feeling none of you Sullivan boys could either," Monroe said with a wide smile. "We'd better get on back to work. Who knows, maybe I'll pry that story out of you today?"

"Not a chance," Colum's eyes met Ellie's pleading ones. "Not even if it comes a ten foot snow and you bury me in it. But we do have a foundation to see about."

A foundation, Douglass thought as she looped her arm in Ellie's, picked up her horse's reins with the other and began to walk home. That's what Ellie and Colum needed. A foundation to build their feelings on. Douglass would shout if her favorite brother stayed in Love's Valley so she'd work hard on helping construct a good solid foundation for Colum and Ellie. She led her horse by the reins, walking beside Ellie, instead of riding.

She and Ellie were engrossed in their own thoughts, not paying a bit of attention to anything around them, when suddenly three men came out of the trees, riding hell bent for leather right at them. Douglass stopped in her tracks, afraid they were going to be killed beneath the horses' hooves. She glanced at Ellie who'd turned whiter than the snow under their feet.

"So," Oscar Wright pulled his horse up right next to Ellie. "Fate has given me another chance at you, woman." He reached down, pushed back the hood from the coat she wore and grabbed her by the hair, yanking her toward him.

Douglass reached up and snatched the gun from the holster on her horse's saddle. Before any one of the three men knew what happened, she had the Colt pointed right at Alvie's chest. "Turn her loose or your friend is dead," she said without so much as a hint of fear.

"There's three of us. You can shoot him if you want but I'll still have this wench with me. This time she's a dead woman," Oscar laughed sarcastically.

One moment he had Ellie by the left arm, hopefully jerking it right out of the socket, the next he was looking into the barrel of a small derringer pointed directly at his nose. He dropped her hair, threw back his head and laughed. "You won't shoot me. You haven't got the guts," he said.

"I will," Ellie tried to control her shaking hands.

"I'd say the odds are that the two of you will be shot," Douglass said. "We might be dead when the firing stops but you'll be running up them steps to the Pearly Gates right behind us. I don't think God is going to knock any jewels from our crowns for taking scum like you out of society, though."

"You going to let her talk to us like that?" Alvie asked.

"I'm going to ride out of here," Oscar said, giving Ellie a solid kick in the stomach and sending her sprawling into the snow. "She won't shoot us."

They kicked their horses and scrambled toward the road just as the derringer fired both times toward them, and Douglass kept firing the Colt until all the ammunition was gone. She hit Alvie in the leg and put a hole through Oscar's hat, she was sure. Damn the rotten luck anyway, she should've hit Alvie square in the back and Oscar's brains should have been blown all the way to the top of the mountain.

"You okay?" She extended a hand toward Ellie who was fighting for breath.

"I'm fine. Did I hit them? Are they dead?" she gasped.

"You came close and did a good job," Douglass assured her with a hug. "One of them is wounded."

While they were still hugging, Monroe pulled Douglass away from Ellie. "Who was that and what happened?" he demanded, checking her for wounds.

Colum took the derringer from Ellie, his own hands trembling as bad as hers.

"Guess that gutter rat Oscar and his two buddies had an idea they could catch two women out by themselves and kill us," she said softly. "Douglass and I both showed them different."

"Sweet baby Jesus," Monroe swore. "Which way did they go? Colum and I'll ride out after them."

"No, let them go. The law can take care of them," Ellie said, her eyes not leaving Colum's. "They've got hiding places you'll never know about. Rats are like that."

"She's right. But from now on, you four women don't even go to the outhouse unless there's two of you. I'll reload the derringer and you keep it with you all the time. Douglass, reload that Colt and watch over them," Colum said.

"I'll place a man in the house with you," Monroe said. "Give me a minute to go to the work site and I'll pick out the best shot."

"You'll do no such thing," Douglass pulled away from him and was already busy reloading the gun. "We need every hand we can beg, borrow, or steal to make my house ready by summer. We're not helpless. We just showed you that. Now go on back and get busy building. We can protect ourselves, even if we are right glad to see you concerned."

"She's right," Colum said, wanting to take Ellie in his arms and wipe away the fear in her eyes, to kiss her until the color came back in her face. "There's men in Texas who'd do battle with a mean old rattlesnake before they would Douglass."

"Tell Mother and Indigo what happened, and make them carry a gun with them every time they go outside," Monroe hugged Douglass one more time.

"I'll do that," Douglass said, still mad at herself because she'd missed.

"He must really hate you," Douglass said when the two men had returned to the work site, looking back over their shoulders every few minutes.

"I've ruined his plans. First to get his hands on my money, then I refused to die, then I came back to Shirleysburg and ruined his chances with the widow there," Ellie held her stomach as she walked.

"You going to be all right?" Douglass asked.

"I'll be fine. He knocked the wind out of me, but the kick itself wasn't as bad as when Turley kicked me," Ellie reassured her, working the kink out of her shoulder bone.

"I won't miss if I ever get another chance. I should've shot him before he started riding away," Douglass said, gritting her teeth.

"I should've put both my bullets in his head, but I hesitated," Ellie said. "It won't happen again. If I see him again, I'll shoot first and answer questions later."

"Why didn't you let Colum hug you?" Douglass asked when they reached the back porch.

"I didn't stop him," Ellie said. "He didn't want to hug me or he would have done so."

Douglass just smiled. Foundations first, then the walls could go up. Just like in her new house.

Chapter Eleven

Except for the occasional snores of the men, all was quiet in the bunkhouse. The weather had held for the past four weeks and the house was coming along right on schedule in spite of the cold days. Twelve foot walls had been built then stood up on the firm foundation. Colum lay awake thinking about the next step: putting down the floor for the second story on top of those walls. Already, he had men crawling around like monkeys in the jungle of skeletal walls. He knew their names now, and they respected him even if they weren't overly friendly. At least they'd learned he was a fair man expecting no more than he was willing to give.

There hadn't been any more snow, thank goodness, and they'd lost only half a day because of rain so far. It had rained hard two Sundays in a row, but come Monday morning the sun peeked out from behind the clouds and work went on. Though it had been colder than a warlock's nose in the middle of an iceberg, the men had simply put on more clothes and kept working, glad for a job that would see them through the lean months of winter.

Colum shut his eyes. Rest was important if he was to keep pace with the men the next day. But sleep didn't settle on him. He sat up and fluffed his pillow, laid back down and

126

tried again, only to find himself staring out the window at the stars and moonlight, thinking of Ellie.

A shadow flitted across the window and instantly he was on his feet, drawing on his trousers and boots, slinging the poncho he'd made in the Blacklog Valley cabin over his head. If Oscar Wright was out there slipping around in the darkness, he'd better bend over, grab his knees and kiss his sorry hind end good-bye, because Colum was headed out the door, strapping the Colt on his hip and bringing a dose of death with him. The tension between the four women had gotten so intense he and Monroe worried that they might begin snatching each other bald-headed if Oscar wasn't caught soon. They all complained about having to go in pairs wherever they went, and the lack of freedom. Indigo, the loudest and shrillest.

He eased out the door in time to catch the culprit's shadow again, only it wasn't Oscar Wright to Colum's disappointment. No, it was Ellie. He'd know that swing of her hips anywhere. Even in the dark with an old blanket poncho thrown over her shoulders and her skirt tails swishing back and forth as she kept a steady pace down the pathway to the new house. Her hair was luminous liquid in the silvery moonlight as it swung loose, the chilly night air picking up strands and twirling them around before letting them fall down her back again. Colum followed a discreet distance behind her, wondering who she was meeting that time of the night. A cold knot of dread filled his belly, one of jealousy like he'd never experienced before. One of the men who worked for him and Monroe must have caught her eye and been paying court to her on the sly. When Colum found out who it was, the man would find himself without a job. He didn't care if it was the best carpenter in his employ. Elspeth Hamilton was a true lady and if a man couldn't court her right out in broad daylight for all the world to see, then he had no business wasting her time. True, she had a tainted reputation now. She'd been in a cabin with three vile men, then traveled with him with no chaperone, either. But no man wasn't going to treat her like anything less than what she was. A true lady.

He gritted his teeth as he kept following her, wishing it would be him at the end of the road where the rendezvous was about to take place. *If wishes were candy, we'd all have a Merry Christmas,* his grandmother's voice came out of nowhere to haunt him. The moon slipped behind a cluster of dark clouds about the time Ellie reached the house. She didn't even pause to look at the huge walls going up, but kept right on walking to the backyard. Colum slipped around the far end of the house and eased to the edge, keeping her in sight. She pushed the drooping branches of the willow tree out of the way and disappeared under them to the trunk of the dormant tree where she sat down on the cold earth, drew her knees up to her chin and wrapped her arms around them, covering her whole body inside the poncho. A person would have to be looking hard to find her in the darkness, wrapped like that.

Soon the clouds moved out of the way and Colum could see her form more clearly, just sitting there, waiting patiently. Pretty soon, he surmised, the man she waited for would come along and they'd embrace. The very idea of seeing that twisted his heart up in a knot so tight he could scarcely breathe but he couldn't leave her there alone. Not with Oscar Wright still on the loose. A week after Douglass and Ellie had had their run in with the man, word had come down from the men who went home on Saturday nights that the three of them had robbed a bank in Chambersburg. He was carrying the tag of being armed and dangerous, and the poster with his picture on it now said dead or alive. Colum considered doing a little bounty hunting, not that he needed the money. Far from it with what his grandfather had left him when he'd died several years before. But it would do Colum's heart good to catch the man and bring him to justice . . . dead or alive.

Half an hour passed and no one appeared. So the scoundrel had stood her up. She'd taken a chance coming out in the night air. True she'd beat the pneumonia bug, but that didn't mean it wouldn't sneak upon her yet, sitting on the cold earth under that willow tree. Or if Oscar Wright was watching the house and Ellie's coming and going, he could easily grab her. What was the woman thinking coming out like that at night? Did she have the little pistol? Anger replaced worry and social standing.

"Just exactly who are you meeting?" He stepped out into the moonlight and demanded.

Ellie jumped at the sound of a voice crackling through the still night air. She had the derringer pointed at the man instinctively as she narrowed her eyes to see exactly who had invaded her space. "Who are you?" She said, her voice quavering barely above a whisper and standing up to squint into the darkness.

"Who do you think might be coming around to meet with you?" Colum asked.

"You!" Ellie put the gun back in her pocket. "Why are you following me?"

"What are you doing out at night? You aren't supposed to go out of the house without someone with you. You know that Oscar is still on the loose! So tell me just who you intended to meet up with here tonight." He began to walk toward her, pushing the weeping bare limbs out of the way as he went.

"I'm meeting no one, Colum. I'm just sick of having Indigo or even Douglass with me all the time. Even Aunt Laura. I love them all, but tonight I couldn't sleep. If I didn't have some time alone I was going to go stark raving mad. What makes you think I'm meeting someone? Who in his right mind would meet me?" she said, huddling back down into her poncho.

"You've got alone time in your room after supper every night," he countered.

"Sure, I do. Indigo is in and out until I'm ready to go to sleep, reminding me that she'll never forgive me if . . ." she stopped dead, thankful that she'd caught herself in time. Sweet baby Jesus, she'd bite her tongue off at the root before she let him know there was even a possibility that she might be in love with him.

"Forgive you for what?" Colum settled down beside her inside his poncho.

"Nothing. She's just always underfoot, that's all. I thought I'd go crazy in the house tonight. So I waited until they were all asleep and came for a walk. Besides I wanted to sit under the willow tree and think," she said.

"About what? You really aren't meeting someone here?" he asked.

"And just who would I be meeting? Get out of the dream world, Colum Sullivan and keep one foot in reality. No one wants me. I've seen the way the women whisper behind their hands when I'm around, and the way the men look at me. Don't you know, I'm tainted goods now. Besides there's still the possibility that I'll wake up one day and be pulling all my hair out, going mad and have to be locked up in the attic for my own protection and for the protection of the Hamilton name," she said.

"Laura wouldn't do that," he said.

"Of course she wouldn't. And if I was going to let that experience ruin my life I would have already done it, don't you think? But it gives the whole community something to talk about, now doesn't it? Elspeth Joy Hamilton, that crazy old maid who was abducted and never did act quite right in the head afterwards. Kind of like Colleen in the story you told me. Who knows, maybe I'll start walking up the lane carrying a bag with strange things in it," she said, a faint grin tickling the corners of her full, sensual mouth.

"They're all crazier than you could be if they think that," he said. "I'm amazed at your stamina and strength. I've seen grown men go through less and come out in far worse shape."

"Thank you," she said. "Women can be strong, Colum. Very strong when they have to be or when they're forced to be. On the outside we are like little rose petals, all soft and sweet, but on the inside we're often made of something a lot tougher because we have to be."

"Ain't that the truth," he nodded. "Think you could tell my sister that she's supposed to be a rose petal some of the time and not an old tough worn-out boot all the time."

"Douglass is the finest rose in all the area," Ellie slapped at him, freeing a hand from under the poncho, "and don't you forget it. She was strong enough to admit it when she made a mistake and strong enough to face the future with Monroe right in the middle of hostile territory. Some of the womenfolks have already begun to forget she's a rebel or that she's Irish and Mexican. She's Monroe's wife and a fine young wife at that."

"Well, pardon me all to pieces," he said. *How do you feel about Irish and Mexicans?* he thought but didn't ask because he was afraid of the answer. "You ready to go back home now? I'll walk with you. And when you've a mind to come out to have some solitary time under the willow tree again, would you please knock on my window? I'll follow discreetly from a distance and leave you alone the whole time. That way I'll be there to protect you."

Ellie just smiled. No, she wouldn't knock on his window. She'd shoot anyone who got in her way with the little gun he'd loaned her, but she would have solitude occasionally even if it caused another war.

He offered his arm and she reached from under the poncho and looped hers through it, not even mildly surprised at the shock that practically glued her to the ground. They covered the distance back to the house in silence, each with their own thoughts. Colum enjoying the warmth deep inside his heart. Ellie fighting the heat in her stomach. When they reached the yard, she slipped her arm out from his and nodded a brief goodnight without speaking. Her mouth was as dry as if she'd just drank a whole bottle of that vile snake oil which was capable of leeching every drop of moisture from inside her lips. If she'd had to speak, they'd just have to come measure her for a long, pine box.

She hadn't gone two steps when she stumbled over a piece of board left in the yard and was on her way to a nasty fall when Colum reached out and grabbed her, dragging her close into his embrace, holding her just a minute longer than necessary. Leaning backward, he flashed her a blinding grin, lighting up the darkness surrounding them. When she was steady, he cupped his face in his hands and looked deeply into her eyes. In the moonlight they were two crystal blue lakes filled with wonder at the closeness of his lips. Lips that claimed hers in the next second. Soul met soul in the middle of the yard that night. Heart melded with heart. And when the kiss ended, neither of them were willing to admit either soul or heart had been affected.

It had just happened because of the near fall.

"So I'll see you tomorrow," he said, his voice so gritty with desire he scarcely recognized it as his.

"Yes, we are butchering tomorrow morning," she said, her own voice high and thin. "Colum, what just happened must not happen again. It wouldn't work, you know. You and I are so different."

"I suppose so," he said, wishing for all the world that Oscar Wright would ride up in the yard right at that moment. He needed to kick something or fight until he couldn't stand any longer. Anything to get the hurt from inside him.

"Goodnight then," she said and disappeared into the house.

Neither of them looked up to see Douglass peeping out

her bedroom window. And Indigo with the drapes drawn back, staring right into the yard.

The building crew was given a half day off that frosty next morning. They could either stay in Shirleysburg and catch up on their own chores or come back to Love's Valley and help with the first butchering of the season. Three steers and six hogs had been fattened for the past couple of weeks in the holding pens.

Monroe and Colum were overseers of the outside work. Shooting the animals. Skinning them and getting the fresh meat ready for the women in the kitchen to cut into the right size pieces or to get ready to go into the smokehouse for the curing process. Laura had decided the night before to pickle half a hog and can several jars of beef for stew as well as cure all twelve hams and pork shoulders, and slabs of pork belly for bacon.

"We'll get the beef in the smokehouse to chill but we'll have to go ahead with the mincemeat today if we're to get the suet, so Ellie and Douglass, you both need to get the raisins and apples ready and boiling. I'll trim the kidneys to get the suet. Recipe is in there," Laura pointed toward a booklet where she kept her time honored instructions. "I see Monroe has already got the cauldron out and set on the andirons for boiling the hog's head and other parts for the souse. Indigo, you can take care of that job. Here, peel these onions and garlic cloves, and add them to the pot with the pork. Keep it stirred well for the next two hours then we'll run it through the ricer and add the other things. We'll have to wait until tomorrow to fry the cracklings. Hope it don't rain and we can do them in two cauldrons out in the yard." Laura kept a running monologue, all the time darting here and there in the kitchen, working harder than three women and twice as fast.

"You were kissing that rebel last night," Indigo hissed at Ellie when she passed her on the way out to the yard.

Ellie blushed but squared her shoulders and got ready for the fight. "What I do is my business, Indigo Hamilton. I'm a full grown woman and I can show affection to whomever I so please."

"I won't have it," Indigo said. "I'll put a stop to it or else."

"What was that all about?" Laura asked, catching only the tail end of the conversation.

"I disobeyed the rules last night," Ellie said, honestly. "I couldn't stand being cooped up with no time by myself to think so after bedtime I went for a walk. Colum saw me and thought I was a trespasser so he followed me to the new house. I like that willow tree in the backyard and I went there to sit and think for a while in solitude. Anyway he walked me home and I stumbled out there in the yard. He grabbed me to prevent the fall and ended up kissing me. I guess Indigo saw it from her window. It wasn't anything and it surely won't happen again."

Douglass smiled and kept peeling apples for the mincemeat. If it didn't happen again she'd carry her piece of pie to Oscar Wright on a silver platter.

"Well, like you said, I expect that's your business," Laura said, biting the inside of her lip to keep back the giggle. "Here comes Colum now with a wheelbarrow full of pork belly. You girls lay aside those apples for now and we'll get the curing on those and send them back to the smokehouse."

"Mornin' ladies," Colum said, leaving the wheelbarrow at the door. "How many of these do you want at a time?"

"Three," Laura said. "Bring them in and you can help us rub in the cure and then take them on to the smokehouse. Eight pounds of salt, two pounds of sugar, two ounces of salt peter," she talked aloud while she measured everything into a huge crock bowl. "Now everyone start rubbing and cover it well. I'll send them out two at a time with Colum. Put them on the shelves with the holes on the south side of the smokehouse. That way when the pickle starts it can run down into the trough below. Once they're out there, Ellie and I will turn them and rub them again every day."

"And in two weeks, we'll have bacon for breakfast," Colum's fingertips brushed against Ellie's when they both reached for fists full of the mixture at the same time. "And might I say, you are looking lovely today, Miss Hamilton."

High color filled Ellie's cheeks. "Thank you, Colum." Now just why did he have to say something like that in front of Aunt Laura and Douglass? Especially right after she'd admitted that he'd kissed her.

"I'll take these two out," Colum picked up the heavy slabs as if they were feather pillows and disappeared out the back door.

"Never happen again?" Douglass poked Ellie in the arm.

"It won't," Ellie declared. "He didn't even mean that compliment. He was just saying it so he could call me Miss Hamilton instead of those other words he used the whole time we were in the cabin. Don't you even recognize sarcasm when you hear it, Douglass Hamilton?"

"What other words?" Douglass rubbed the mixture into another slab of bacon.

"*Querida, a ghra,* her English royalty," Ellie said, the words sounding flat and not at all like they did when they came out of Colum's mouth with his Texas drawl spiced up with that faint Irish brogue. "I'm probably not saying them right, though. They slid off his tongue like the stories about the fairies and the one about the willow tree."

"He called you *a ghra?*" Douglass' eyes widened. It meant 'my love' in Irish. That endearment was saved for when people were engaged.

"Some of the time. Mostly *querida* or *her English royalty,*" Ellie said.

"Monroe referred to me a few times as her Irish majesty. So did those mean men who kidnapped me," Douglass said. "Did he tell you what *a ghra* means?"

"Yes, sweetheart and darling, according to him. One in

Mexican. One in Irish and the English majesty was just to make me mad," Ellie said.

"Got two more ready?" Colum poked his head in the back door.

"Yes, we do," Laura said. "By the time you get those out there we'll have these final two done and then you can get on back to helping bring in the hams."

"Yes, ma'am," Colum drawled, letting his fingertips brush against Ellie's again just so he could enjoy that sensation of his whole insides going to mush. Someday in Bowie County, Texas, he was going to find a woman who had the same effect on him.

At noon the work stopped long enough for everyone to get a chunk of fresh beef liver fried in onions, baked sweet potatoes and slabs of homemade bread. They ate in the bunkhouse at the long tables where the hired help were served every day. Douglass sat beside Monroe and filled him in on the flirtations of Ellie and Colum in soft whispers when the conversation got loud enough between the others that she could do it without being heard. Indigo sat beside her mother and thought of new ways to kill Colum Sullivan. She'd throw his sorry old hide into the souse pot and boil the flesh from his bones, but it would no doubt poison the souse and she did like it with her pancakes in the winter mornings. Maybe she'd hit him on the head with his own hammer and bury him under the rose bushes in the garden. No, couldn't do that. The roses would wilt and die by feeding on the rotting remains of a rebel.

Colum and Ellie sat across the table from each other. Dishes were passed. Hands touched. Eyes met and twinkled.

Claude sat on one side of Ellie, Fred Zimmerman on the other. The flirtations and sparks passing to and fro across the table didn't escape their watchful eye. Claude figured what went on between Elspeth Hamilton and Colum Sullivan wasn't one bit of his business. He'd agreed to work for Colum and the man had been fair. Claude still kept his cool distance, not wanting to be thought a rebel lover by his friends and neighbors, but still respecting the man for his fairness with the men Monroe had hired. Colum didn't strut around being the boss of the project. No sir, he rolled up his sleeves and worked just as hard and sometimes longer hours than any of them. While they played cards at night or told tall tales, he studied the plans and made a list of things that had to be done the next day. So if he enjoyed a bit of flirtation with Ellie, then Claude wasn't faulting him one bit. Not that anything would ever come of it anyway. Ellie Hamilton would be an old maid. Pretty as she was, no one would take a chance on her. Not with the possibility she'd go crazy, nor with the very real possibility that something had gone on in that cabin. Claude just couldn't see Turley, Alvie, or Oscar walking away without having his way with her.

Fred's nose snarled at the sight of that Irishman making eyes at Miss Hamilton across the table. Lord have mercy, she must truly be touched in the head to even look at that man. True enough, he was a fair boss, just like he said he'd be, but that didn't mean he could carry on with one of Love's Valley's own. Not that Fred would step up and ask to take Elspeth for a Sunday ride after church. No, sir, he wouldn't do that. Everyone knew what had happened and he wasn't going to be the laughing stock of Huntingdon County. But as a neighbor and friend to the family, he sure owed it to her to give her a talking to if Monroe wasn't going to do his duty by his cousin.

"If I might have a few minutes of your time, Miss Hamilton," Fred said as they were leaving the tables. "In private," he added, a slow blush crawling up his neck.

Sweet Lord, Fred Zimmerman was going to ask permission to court me, Ellie thought as she nodded slightly. Fred, who was at least ten years older than she was, who took care of his aging mother who was nothing less than a shrew. Fred, with a tongue almost as sharp as his mother's and who dipped snuff.

"Could we just step up here beside the souse pot while Indigo is helping remove the dinner dishes? That way no one will think anything amiss," he said, holding the bunkhouse door open for her.

Double sweet Lord, she rolled her eyes toward the winter blue sky. Not only was he wanting to court her but he was wanting to do it on the sly so no one would know. What was it the Good Book said in Isaiah? Something about where the body was the vultures would gather. Looked like the first of the buzzards had spotted a rotten reputation and was zeroing in for a tasty midnight rendezvous.

Ellie picked up the stirring paddle and without watching Fred fill his lower lip with powdered snuff, began to stir the souse mixture, the aromatic aroma of onions and garlic filling the air.

"Monroe should be taking care of this, but since he ain't, then I feel it's my honor bound duty to step in and tell you about that Colum Sullivan," Fred didn't mince words but rather dove right into the problem at hand.

Thank you God, Ellie sent up an instant prayer of gratitude. *At least he's not going to ask me to meet him in the middle of the night for a few snuff tasting kisses.*

"What's your problem with Colum? Has he not been fair as a boss?" Ellie asked.

"No, the man is fair even if he is a rebel. But any blind fool could see that he's making eyes at you, Miss Hamilton, and that will not do. No, it will not do at all. You must put a stop to such shenanigans right now. We won't stand for such a thing," Fred said.

"Why?" Ellie asked.

"First of all he's a rebel and he fought on the wrong side of the war. Second he's an Irishman. A lowdown Irishman. You don't know anything about them, but they're not like us. They . . . well, suffice it to say they're just low class. And third, he's a Mexican, which is worse than an Irishman. He's got his eye on your money, just like that Oscar Wright, and you'd do well to heed what I'm saying," Fred said, spitting out a stream of brown snuff on the ground so close to the fire that it sizzled.

"I think I'm old enough and wise enough to handle my own affairs," Ellie told him coldly. "I do believe you have work to do and I know I do so we will end this conversation right now."

"You ain't the same since the kidnapping. I reckon I can understand that you'd think you'd have to settle for the likes of Colum Sullivan, what given the fact that you ain't pure no more, but you need to understand that he ain't acceptable, not even for someone like you," Fred didn't budge.

"Go away and don't you ever speak to me again," Ellie hissed at him.

"What did you just say about my cousin?" Monroe and Colum appeared behind him just in time to catch the last of the conversation.

"I said she didn't need to think she had to settle for Colum Sullivan just because she ain't pure no more," Fred said.

"I think maybe you and I'd better step out behind the bunkhouse and take care of this matter," Colum said. "No one is going to talk about Ellie Hamilton like that. You don't know what she's been through and you have no right to cast such accusations at her."

"I don't think so," Monroe put up a hand. "Bill leaves in ten minutes to go into town for tomorrow's supplies from the sawmill. Fred, you pack whatever you own in that bunkhouse and be on that wagon. Your job is finished here."

"Good," Fred sneered. "I ain't working for nobody who can't appreciate the fact that I was just being honest. Wake up and face the facts, Monroe. What I said is just the truth."

Colum's fist answered him.

One hard hit and Fred was on the ground, the wind knocked solidly from his lungs, his nose pouring blood.

"You'll be sorry you did that," he mumbled through his hand, trying to catch the blood.

"Get on out of here before I give you another dose," Monroe said. "Now, Colum let's get to work."

"I'm so sorry Ellie," Colum stayed behind long enough to apologize. "They're just small-minded, evil people if they think that of you."

Ellie nodded as she turned her back and went toward the back door without looking back. So it had finally been put in words. That's the way the whole community viewed her. Tears filled her blue eyes but she bit her lip and refused to let them surface. Why cry, when it was the truth, just like Fred said. She had the name without the game. She'd never know what it was like to awake in a man's arms in the early morning hours. She'd never know a love like Aunt Laura and Uncle Harrison shared, or Douglass and Monroe.

"Whatever is wrong with you?" Douglass asked when Ellie rushed into the kitchen, picked up a knife and began to peel more apples for mincemeat.

"Facing the truth is hard, isn't it? I've just been insulted. Fred Zimmerman has been fired. Colum took up for me but he knows now without a doubt what people are saying about me," Ellie said.

"Colum's not going to give a whit what people say," Douglass patted Ellie on the back.

"Yes, he will," Indigo jumped on the band wagon. "He's just playing with your affections, Ellie. You're vulnerable and he's taking advantage of you."

"I told you not to talk about my brother like that," Douglass bowed up to Indigo.

"And I'm telling the bunch of you that we've got too much work to do to be bickering," Laura said. "Indigo, get back out there to tend the souse, and watch that smart mouth or I will slap it for you. I don't care if you're grown. If you act like a child, you'll be treated like one. A grown woman knows when to keep her views to herself. What's done is done. Work and lots of it will take our mind off what was said. We'll get it all in the proper perspective by keeping our hands busy and giving our minds time to work everything out. Ellie, don't worry about it. Douglass, forgive Indigo's rashness. Now go to work."

Keep my hands busy and think it through, Ellie thought. *Even when the work is finished, it won't change me, nor will it change the fact not even an Irishman would want me now.*

Chapter Twelve

Christmas morning dawned with the onset of a blizzard. Since the day was on a Tuesday, Monroe had given the construction crew both Monday and Tuesday off to spend the holidays with their families. He and Colum were both glad that the house was in the dry now with the roof on, the outside walls up, covered with lap siding and painted white, and the porch pillars all set in place even if they hadn't gotten painted just yet. Lathing and plaster would have to be applied to the inner walls and the slow job of finish carpentry done in the next few months, but at least the men could work inside every day and didn't have to depend on the sun shining.

Colum awoke early that morning to snow blowing so hard that he couldn't even see the main house from the bunkhouse. After a trip out to help with the early morning chores, he threw his poncho over his head, gathered all the presents he'd bought into the center of a blanket and braced himself for the onslaught as he opened the door.

He was not disappointed. If anything the wind had picked up. Forget whistling down the valley. It was howling like a baby calf that had been separated from its mother. That soft snowflakes could actually sting when they hit his face was a mystery, but they surely did. By the time he reached the kitchen door and flung it open, snow covered him, sticking even to his eyelashes.

The thought of a warm Christmas in Texas where he and his brothers played a game of baseball in the backyard after dinner almost brought tears to his frozen eyes. Douglass Esmerelda had best never ask him for a favor again. He didn't care if she begged until angels gave away blocks of ice . . . in hell. If it involved living in Love's Valley during another winter, the answer would be no. No, that wasn't right. The answer would be definitely no—with no discussion involved.

"And do we have St. Nick?" Laura reached for the blanket bag of gifts. "I'll put these in the living room. When everyone is up and has had breakfast we'll do an exchange."

"Thank you," he said, peeling out of the poncho and hanging it on a nail inside the door beside Ellie's. She'd really taken to that old thing he'd made her in the cabin, wearing it every day when she went outside. He dusted the snow from his hair and eyes, kicked off his wet boots, leaving them beside the door and padding through the dining room into the living room in his socks.

"Was that cinnamon rolls I smelled back in the kitchen?" he asked Laura.

"Sure was. Christmas tradition. On Christmas morning the children could sleep as long as they wanted and they always had fresh baked cinnamon rolls for breakfast. It's a leisure time without worry over chores since Harrison and I always did them early. Since he's been gone it's the one day I do them alone. At least most years. This year I had some help from a mighty handsome Texan," she smiled. She'd gotten up before daylight to put out bread dough to rise, then go to the barn and milk the two cows, feed the livestock and take care of the rest of the morning chores. She'd found Colum already up and about, horses fed and enjoying fresh, clean stalls, pigs grunting in the hog house as they snorted down their morning swill, and the chickens pecking at grain he'd strewn in the hen house. All she had to do was milk the two cows while he finished up and went back to the bunkhouse to change into his best suit of clothes for the holiday.

"If I'd known there was going to be cinnamon rolls, I'd had them two cows milked, too," he smiled.

He'd won her heart in the past weeks and she sincerely hoped Ellie woke up and realized what she'd been very busy shunning. Since Fred Zimmerman said what he did that day she'd withdrawn. The new, sassy Ellie had gone back into a shell and refused to emerge. She did her work quietly, laughed at times with Douglass, tolerated Indigo's smart mouth, but she steered clear of Colum Sullivan.

Indigo wandered sleepily down the stairs first, sneering at Colum as she passed him sitting in an overstuffed chair beside the fireplace. Her mother was serving him a plate of cinnamon rolls and a cup of coffee, saying that anyone who'd already put in a morning's work deserved to be waited on a bit.

"Merry Christmas to you, Indigo," Colum said cheerily. The ice queen of the Hamilton clan hated him. Laura had come around and was his precious friend. Monroe, as close as a brother. Ellie, well, Ellie was examining her own dreams right now. The Irish in him recognized that, even thought the Mexican in him wanted results today. He'd wait. It might take a couple of years before she was finished thinking and then he'd come back to Love's Valley one fine summer and see what might happen. But Indigo, now there was a piece of work. Ice cold vinegar ran in her veins instead of warm blood.

Indigo barely answered him with a shrug. Christmas morning was spoiled the minute she saw him eating her special breakfast, sitting in her living room beside her fire place and her Christmas tree. The only thing she could be happy about was that Ellie would be down soon and if she hurried she could bring her own breakfast to the living room and watch her shun the rebel. Now that was a wonderful Merry Christmas idea!

Monroe and Douglass both had a gleam in their eye as they brought their breakfast into the living room to join Colum and Indigo. Someday Colum would have a relationship like that. One where he could look across the room at his wife and they could carry on a conversation without saying a single word.

"Merry Christmas, my brother," Douglass stopped long enough to kiss Colum on the forehead before she joined Monroe on the settee. "And to you, too, Indigo."

"Same from the man she's married to," Monroe kissed her on the cheek.

Ellie, or at least the shell of the woman he'd met in that cabin brought her plate to the living room and sat down in the corner, far away from everyone. She nibbled at the edges of the hot roll without tasting a single bite of it. When had she lost that woman she'd found up there in that cabin? That was easy to answer. The day Fred Zimmerman said those ugly things. Like Aunt Laura had said, she'd drowned herself in work, thinking the whole time she kept her hands busy, and the only thing she'd accomplished was burying herself under a pile of work and mental pain.

"This appears to be a new tradition, but then maybe it should be," Laura brought her own breakfast in to join her family. "We've got a new member in our family. Welcome to your first Hamilton Christmas, Douglass. So we'll make it a new tradition to eat in the living room on Christmas morning."

"Thank you, Momma Laura," Douglass said respectfully. "I'm glad to be here. Even though I miss all my other brothers this morning, I'm glad for the love I've found here."

"You didn't get it from me," Indigo said. "And that brother you begged into staying doesn't get any either."

Something snapped inside Ellie, bringing her out of a near catatonic state. Indigo had done nothing for the past two months but berate the Sullivans, both Douglass and Colum. Neither of them deserved such crude and rude treatment.

"Shut up!" Ellie stood up so fast her chair fell backwards, the plate with her hot roll crashed onto the floor with a bang, and her cup of tea followed it, all of it lying there in a mess of sugar, wet tea, and broken china. "You've not got a bit of Christmas charity in your heart, Indigo Hamilton. You're selfish, spoiled, and never had to face anything unpleasant in your life. You should be licking that man's boots for rescuing me if nothing else instead of being so hateful. And you know down deep in your heart you admire Douglass for everything she's done. So hush and stop spoiling her first Christmas with us and possibly Colum's only Christmas with us."

"Don't you talk to me like that. The townfolks are right. That whole episode has made you crazy. And I have had to face unpleasant things, too. You lost your parents, but they were my favorite aunt and uncle. All three of my brothers went to war and I had to worry about them coming home safe," Indigo was on her feet and inches from Ellie's nose.

Laura started across the floor to put a stop to the fight, but Monroe put a hand on her arm and shook his head. Bowing to the wisdom in his smile, she sat down on the settee beside her son.

"Let them take care of it. Indigo needs the lesson and it looks like Ellie is finally shaking off the shell she's been hiding in since butchering day," he whispered.

Ellie snapped her hands on her hips and glared at her cousin. "Those things should make you mature, not act like a child. And crazy can be cured and I am cured, Indigo Hamilton. Meanness and bitterness like you are eat up with ain't got no cure," Ellie said barely below an out and out shout. Faith and saints above, she'd never screamed in her life. Ladies didn't do that. Her mother would turn over in her grave if she could hear her only daughter yelling like a fish wife at her cousin.

But it felt so danged good.

Emotions, be they love, disgust, arguments, were wonderful. Freedom from apathy soured through her veins and she loved the feeling. Passion replaced indifference in her heart. She was Elspeth Joy Hamilton and she would, by all the saints above, stand up for what she believed in from that moment through eternity. And if Indigo thought she would bow under the pressure of contradiction, then she'd better wake up and smell the horse manure, because it was going to get smelly living in the house with Ellie from now on.

"You're the one ruining Christmas," Indigo said.

"I'm the one trying to keep you from ruining the holiday for all of us. If you can't be civil to our family, then maybe you'd better be working as hard as I have these past weeks. Aunt Laura said hard work would make the mind think about things and it sure enough does. So maybe you'd better do a couple of days work out in the barn, shoveling manure until your hands bleed. Maybe that would make you grow up and act like the woman you think you are," Ellie said.

Colum grinned. How many times had he and his brothers, along with Douglass, had similar arguments. Mercy, if it weren't for the snow trying to bury them he might have felt right at home. Rather than embarrassing him, he felt like jumping up and dancing a jig in the middle of the living room floor. Ellie was back. His Ellie. The one who'd argued about everything in that cabin. The one who'd walked down that mountain with him. Who'd trusted him to sleep beside her in the same bed. The one who had captured his heart and made him fall in love with her.

Whoa! Wait a minute, he argued with himself, the smile fading and wrinkles covering his brow as he frowned. He could appreciate her spunk. Could even admire her beauty. He could make plans to come back in a couple of years and see what might happen. But love her today? That was some pretty serious thinking. Maybe he needed to go out to the barn and shovel manure all day so he could think that idea through.

"You are a pigheaded fool," Indigo hissed, uncomfortable in the argument now. Sure she liked Douglass, admired her more than anyone would ever know for the way she'd carved out a place for herself not only in Love's Valley but in the surrounding community in the very worst of circumstances. But she wasn't going to tell her that. And she absolutely abhorred Colum. All his handsome, charming ways trying to wiggle into the family by pretending to care about Ellie. No sane man would want a woman like Ellie, not now. No sane woman who had three cousins who fought for the Union and who'd lost her parents and home to the rebels would want a man like Colum. And that wasn't even mentioning the fact of the Irish and Mexican blood.

"And you are a little girl," Ellie said, not backing down an eyelash.

"He won't marry you. He's no better than Oscar. He's just messing with you, kissing you out there in the yard in the dark of night. You don't see him coming around in the light of day courting you proper do you?" Indigo slung in her face.

Colum started to stand, but Douglass shook her head. Indigo might have just said a mouth full of stinky words, but it wasn't really his fight. It was Ellie's, just like it had been hers so many times when she locked horns with her brothers.

Ellie clamped her mouth shut and glared at Indigo for several moments, then simply raised her hand and slapped fire into her cheek. "My personal life is none of your concern from this day forth, little lady, and you'd do well not to judge everyone by your own half bushel."

"Mother, she hit me," Indigo said as she held her stinging face.

"And you deserved it," Laura said. "Now you go out in the kitchen and think about your attitude. I'll give you five minutes and then we're going to have presents in this room, with or without you."

"One more thing before you go to the kitchen," Ellie said.

She marched across the room where Colum was sitting, amazement written all over his face. She brushed the tail of her night rail and robe back and sat down in his lap. She cupped his face in her hands and kissed him soundly right in front of God, Laura and the rest of the family. Sliding her tongue over his bottom lip and nipping it just slightly with her teeth heated up her insides like she'd built a raging hot fire there. The feeling was absolutely delicious. "If you've a mind to come courting, you might remember that kiss. I'm going out in the kitchen to think for five minutes now before we exchange our gifts, too. Come on Indigo, let's go make up and put on another pot of coffee to share after we have gifts," she patted Colum's cheek and swept out of the room with Indigo in tow.

"Whew," Colum whistled through his teeth. "Merry Christmas to me."

"I'd say so. I guess she's worked hard enough to think it through," Laura laughed.

"It's wonderful," Douglass all but clapped her hands.

"Don't you be going getting ideas. A man can pay court to a lovely woman without it getting serious," Colum said staunchly.

"Yes, he can," Monroe agreed.

"Thanks, brother," Colum wiped his brow. When had the room gotten so blistering hot?

It took fifteen minutes for Ellie and Indigo to make up in the kitchen and return to the living room. Indigo marched right up to Colum who was leaning against the wall on the far side of the hot room, trying to keep a silly grin off his face.

"The fact that Ellie finds you the least bit attractive is a total mystery to me. That she would lower herself to kiss you in front of the whole family shows that she's not got her right mind, but I'm not living in her shoes and I don't have her heart, thank the good Lord above. Now we'll have Christmas if Momma is ready. I haven't really changed my mind about you but I will tolerate you until spring when I fully well expect you to leave Love's Valley," she said.

"You are forgiven," Colum said with only the faintest hint of humor in his deep voice.

"I didn't apologize," Indigo stuck her nose in the air and winked at Ellie.

"Someday in the future, I see a world where women are going to vote, hold office in the government and maybe someday, there'll even be a woman president," Ellie said crossing the room to loop her arm in Colum's. "That's a long time away and I don't suppose I'll be alive to see the womenfolks as liberated as the slaves. But today I'm going to liberate this woman. Today I'm going to court you, Colum Sullivan."

"Women in government offices," Monroe chuckled. "And I suppose you'll be a general in the next war, Ellie?"

"No, but my granddaughters might. Because I'm going to have a family someday. I've decided that all the wicked tongues in Huntingdon County aren't going to control my life another moment. Now let's see what we've got hiding in the presents under the tree? Did you buy me something pretty, Colum? I surely hope so because I made you something lovely and since I'm courting you, I expect you to like it," she said.

Poor Colum Sullivan was completely tongue tied as he let the blond-haired vixen lead him across the room, shove him into a chair and then perch herself on the arm beside him. Every nerve in his body was at attention, wondering just how he'd gotten himself in this pickle. There was no way Elspeth would leave Love's Valley even if they did get serious, and there was no way he was staying.

Ellie gave Colum a lovely scarf she'd knitted for him in soft brown wool yarn, just the color of his eyes, she told him when he opened it, then laughed at the deep red color filling his handsome face. She squealed when she opened her real poncho he'd had imported from DeKalb. It was bright red plaid with fringe and a hood. Throwing her arms around his neck, she kissed him soundly for the second time, and then modeled it for the whole family.

"And do I get a real Leine-and-Brat for my birthday which is on Valentine's Day?" she asked.

"You might," Colum said, a sheepish grin splitting his face, showing off perfectly even white teeth. How did she know he'd already commissioned it to be made for her as a going away present? Hopefully, it would be ready by her birthday. For another one of those kisses that knocked his socks off his feet, he would have her a dozen ponchos and Leine-and-Brats made in every tartan plaid available.

When all the rest of the gifts were opened, Monroe cleared his throat and took Douglass's hand in his. "We've got an announcement and we've saved it for today to share with you. Douglass is expecting our first child. It'll be here this summer. We hope our house is ready by then."

All melee broke loose. Laura hugged and cried. Her first grandchild. Even Indigo let go of her prejudice and hugged Douglass. Ellie literally danced a jig in her pink flannel night rail covered with a bright red plaid poncho. A new baby to bring life to the valley. What a wonderful present! By this time next year she'd have a lovely little baby to hold and spoil. A girl. It had to be a girl that she could dress in frills and laces.

"Of course, we want a boy," Monroe said.

"But we're not naming him Herman," Douglass laughed. She still hated her husband's first name. It reminded her of the old wino derelict who scared the bejesus out of her and the other children in DeKalb, Texas. She remembered the first time she heard Laura call him by his whole name and how funny the look on his face had been.

"Or Colum Eduardo," she caught the dreamy look in Colum's eye. "I don't care if you did succumb to my begging and stay in this winter wonderland to build my house."

"Maybe you'll name him Hermana if he's a girl," Indigo giggled, caught up in the happy mood.

"We're naming him Michael Milford if he's a boy. And calling him Ford," Monroe said.

"And if he's a girl?" Ellie asked.

"Maybe she'll be Michael Milford. I grew up with a boy's name and it didn't kill me," Douglass said. "We could call her Millie. Actually we haven't thought of a girl's name but we will before summer."

"Something Irish," Colum said.

"Lord, I hope not. It'll be something I can't even pronounce, like *a ghra!*" Ellie said, a look of pure disgust on her face.

"You don't like the Irish?" Colum asked.

"No, I do not," Ellie said. "They're a hardheaded lot of people. Couldn't knock sense in them with a frying pan."

"Then maybe she'll use a Mexican name for my new niece," Colum said defensively. What happened to the sweet woman who gave him a lovely scarf and two kisses on Christmas?

"Lord, I hope not," Ellie said. "I don't like Mexicans either. They're hotheaded. You'd think Indigo had Mexican blood as fast as she is to get mad about any little thing."

"You want to go back to the kitchen?" Indigo narrowed her eyes.

"Well, I'm both so why are you courting me?" Colum ignored Indigo and glared at Ellie. If she couldn't accept him for what he was, then be hanged if he'd stand still to be courted or court either one.

"Danged if I know. Guess it's because you kiss right good," she said with a giggle and disappeared up the stairs to change into the dress she had laid out for the rest of the day.

"Me thinks you've met your match," Douglass said.

"Me thinks I'm going to run home to Texas as soon as this blizzard is over. I bet I could jump off that mountain over there," he nodded out the front door, "and slide all the way home without even stopping for supper."

"Chicken," Douglass goaded him. "You going to fight for her or with her?"

"Pretty scary ain't it," Colum said seriously. "I like Ellie. Like her spirit and her fire now that she's worked through her problems, but honestly Douglass, she's not going to Texas, and we both know it, so courting is all we're going to do. It's a dead end road."

"We'll see," Laura said quietly. "Now Douglass and Indigo, let's go check on that ham in the oven and leave these menfolks to their coffee and most likely discussions of politics. They'd better enjoy their exclusive time in that field if Ellie is right. To think my relative might be the first woman president. That's something, ain't it?"

Lost in his own thinking, Colum suddenly wished he had a hammer in his hands to keep himself busy so he could think. Today he'd flirt with Ellie, there was that much sentimental Irish and passionate Mexican in him. But what would tomorrow bring?

Ellie dressed quickly in the blue dress she'd laid out for the special day. Who'd have thought she'd toss aside all those depressing moods so quickly. *Thank you Indigo for riling me up,* she thought as she checked her reflection in the mirror. She didn't look crazy even if she had acted like a wanton, crazy fool today. Fighting with Indigo in front of other people. Kissing Colum, not once but twice. What had come over her?

"Well, whatever it was, I hope it stays," she said. Spring might bring nothing but a big heartache when Colum went home to Texas, but everyone in the community would know that she wasn't sitting home fretting herself into gray hair.

Chapter Thirteen

Delicate white snow flowers felt the sun ray's warmth and put up minty green leaves in spite of weather hovering around the freezing mark. When the leaves survived they put on the first show of the year with a profusion of tiny flowers, low to the ground but serving as the harbinger of spring. If Ellie looked close enough she could see the first nubbins on the weeping willow that would eventually bring forth green leaves. She remembered the story all too well of the weeping willow tree planted on the high cliffs in County Cork, Ireland at the head of two stubborn people's graves. Patrick, who'd been too stubborn to come back home after he'd amassed his fortune, for fear that his only love, Colleen would be married to another. Colleen, who realized her mistake in throwing Patrick's true love back in his face, and had no idea where to find him, so she waited until he came back to her in a pine box.

Did their spirits unite in the afterlife, she wondered? Did they sit beneath the willow tree every spring and watch the leaves turn green? Ellie drew her poncho around her. Rays of the warm sun might bring on snow flowers and the promise of leaves on the willow tree, but the cold north wind told her winter wasn't quite finished yet. All was quiet at the con-

struction site. The big white house was finished on the outside, windows were in place and Douglass had even begun
to think about flowers. She'd said she wanted her house to
look like an Irish village home with flowers of every kind
and description flowing from beds and inviting people to
come by for a cup of tea and a visit.

Ellie doubted that many Irish village houses were six bedroom, two-story white mansions with six pillars holding up
the front porch. But if Douglass wanted a riot of flowers then
she'd help her plant them when warm weather really arrived.
Marigolds, petunias, ferns, roses, larkspur, holly hock, sweet
william were all there for the cutting in Aunt Laura's yard.

"What are you thinking about?" Colum asked from the
other end of the swing hung on the back porch. He'd forgot-
ten who courted who these days. First Ellie said she was
courting him to liberate women from having to sit back and
wait on a man to notice them, then he was bringing her little
gifts. The first snow flower blossom pressed between the
pages of a book. A lace edged handkerchief he found at the
general store with a violet embroidered on one of corners.
He wished for a seashell but somehow the mountains of
Love's Valley didn't produce many seashells.

"I'm thinking about Patrick and Colleen again," she said.
"Was your brother Patrick named for that one?"

"No," he reached across the swing and took her hand in
his. It fit there well, albeit it was not a dainty, little hand
dwarfed by his own big one. Ellie wasn't petite, nor was she
a shrinking violet. She came just shy of looking him right in
the eye when they were standing, and she cut a fine figure
when she donned her fitted shirt waist and skirts that nipped
in at her tiny waist, showing off an ample bosom. "No,
Patrick was named for my father's father, Patrick Cordona is
his full name. The Cordona is my Mexican grandfather's
middle name."

"Was your grandfather the poor Irish potato farmer's son
who came to America to find his fortune and get away from

the love of his life?" she asked trying to find a real live thread somewhere in the story.

"No, my grandfather stayed in Ireland until his death. My father, Michael, came to America to buy horses from the Montoya family. My grandfather, Patrick, was one of those rarities, a wealthy Irishman with a big horse farm. Michael was his only child so he wasn't really happy when he fell in love with Mary Margaret Montoya and decided to stay in America. Grandfather came to visit every other year until he died, though, and he and my Mexican grandfather were great friends," Colum used his thumb to draw gentle circles on the soft skin on the top of Ellie's hand.

A slow heat started in Ellie's stomach and rambled all the way through her body, warming her, turning her legs into jelly and her insides to a quivering mass of hot mush. How was she ever going to survive without Colum?

"We're like them, you know," she whispered.

"And how's that?" He leaned across the swing to kiss her on the cheek, amazed every time he did it at how soft her skin was.

"I've loved the courting, Colum. The little presents. The walks like this on Sunday after dinner. Sitting with you on the swing. Watching the house grow like our feelings for each other. First there was the foundation. That's kind of like you rescuing me and leaving behind your saddle to carry me to the church when I fainted. It's even more like you knocking Fred Zimmerman into the dirt for being so nasty. It's backing off and letting me find myself those weeks after that, and not stepping in when Indigo and I were fighting. Which by the way, she's still totally against us even courting, but she's learning to bite her tongue a little better now. I think she might be growing up," Ellie said, gripping his hand tighter in hers.

Colum waited. Something told him he wasn't going to like where this conversation was headed, but Ellie had the right to say her piece before he said anything at all.

"Then the walls went up. That Christmas Day when I kissed you and defied all social laws by saying I was going to court you. We built something that day on the foundation. These past weeks we've put some finish on the outside, getting to know each other. And now we're working on the inside, the heart and soul side. But we're like Patrick and Colleen. I heard you and Monroe talking to the men yesterday morning. In six weeks, the house will be finished with the extra hands you've hired and you're going home to Texas," she said.

Colum still waited. Could be that she wasn't descended from English royalty at all, but from Irish roots, with that much philosophizing.

Ellie cleared her throat, swallowing down the lump. "Even though you aren't a poor carpenter from the farm over in the next valley, and I'm not the rich landowner's daughter, we're like them. You're going to go to your Texas which is like Patrick's America. I'm going to stay here."

She stopped long enough that Colum figured she'd finished. "Why?"

"Why are you going to Texas or why am I staying here?" she asked.

"Both," he said.

"You are going to Texas because that's where your heart is, Colum. You could no more survive in my valley than I could in your flat land. And I'm staying because this is where my heart is. The jest of the story is that we are starcrossed lovers. It isn't going to happen, Colum. I care about you more than you'll ever know, and like the house, when we look deep into our hearts, to the very corner of the attic, I know you share those feelings. But it's not going to work out. We'll just have to be adults and realize that what we have shared is just a moment in the big hour glass of time," she said.

"Spit it out, Ellie. What exactly are you saying?" Colum let go of her hand.

"I'm saying that I'm going to get up off this swing and walk back to the house alone. I'm going to leave you sitting here just like Colleen did Patrick. I don't want you to try to talk me out of it. Don't make a rash offer like telling me I can go to Texas with you. I can't. Don't ask me why. I just can't. I've thought about it. Even thought I could tell you that I'd live anywhere with you, but I can't," she said. "So this is our good-bye. I'll treasure the time we've had and I'm beholden to you forever for awakening my heart to what can be."

"It just can't be with me, is that what you're saying?" Colum asked. The passionate part of his heart wanted to offer to stay in Love's Valley with her, but the sensible part convinced him to keep his mouth shut. Why should he give up his life for her? Why couldn't she give up her love of this part of the country for him? If she truly loved him, Irish, Mexican, Rebel and all, she'd be willing to go anywhere with him. Their story truly was like the one he had made up concerning the willow tree. She wasn't willing to give up her world for his and as much as he'd come to love Ellie, he wouldn't propose to a woman who wasn't willing to take the whole package of Colum Sullivan. Texas and all.

"Good-bye, Colum," she bent down and brushed a kiss across his lips.

"Good-bye, Ellie," he whispered but he didn't reach out to draw her down in his lap for a real kiss. It had been a pleasant time during their courting. Now he'd just have to finish the next six weeks and go home. The only difference in their story and the one that he'd invented was that they'd never bring Colum Sullivan back to Love's Valley to bury him. If Ellie could give him up with a brief kiss and a tearless good-bye, then she'd no doubt find another love. She was a good-looking woman and there were plenty of men in the community who'd come calling now that she'd proven her mind wasn't affected. He'd never marry, though. He'd be just like the poor Irishman's son in his story. He'd go home, build another fortune on the one his grandfather left him, and leave it all to his nieces and nephews. Had the character in his story been a real man, Colum knew exactly how he would have felt that day as he watched his Colleen walk away from him. No more than Patrick could love another when his heart belonged to Colleen, could Colum let another woman into his life when his heart belonged to her English royalty, his *querida,* his *a ghra.* He left the swing, pushed back the limbs of the willow tree and laid his head against the tree's trunk. Tears flowed down his cold cheeks, dripping onto the cold earth.

Ellie kept her own tears at bay until she reached the house. By the time she got halfway up the stairs, her back was still ramrod straight and her chin held high, but tiny rivulets of salty tears bathed her face and dropped from her cheekbones onto the poncho. She might love one rebel, but to go to Texas and love the whole Confederate way of life was quite another thing. Father John often mentioned the rites of absolution. The total forgiveness of sins. Ellie would have to embrace total absolution of the past to love Colum. That involved trust so deep it became unconditional love, and love so deep was an absolution of all that went on before. She couldn't do it. She just couldn't. Besides, even though she'd faced the wrath of the community surrounding Love's Valley when she began courting Colum, she'd at least proven she wasn't going to let the ordeal she'd survived scar her. To go to Texas where she'd be a Yankee from the wrong side of the world, where she'd be an English woman in an Irish household, where she'd be shunned by his family would be more than she could bear.

Absolution? There wasn't that much trust or love left after the war that had just been fought.

"What on earth has happened?" Douglass met her on the stairs.

"It's over. Colum and I are not courting each other anymore," Ellie said between sobs.

"What did that fool Mexican do? I'll take this up with him

right now and he'll be on his knees apologizing in the next five minutes or else I'll take a hammer to his thick skull," Douglass crossed her arms over her chest, her blue eyes glittered in anger. Just when it was beginning to look so good he ruined it.

"It wasn't him," Ellie said. "I can't go on loving him, Douglass. My heart is going to break when he leaves and I cannot go to Texas. I just can't. It might as well break now and begin to scar over as wait until then."

"Are you saying that you ended it?" Douglass said. "But you love him."

"Yes, I do, but I could never ask him to stay here and I won't leave. Besides it won't work. Not now. Not in this lifetime," Ellie said.

"You're saying you intend to fall out of love?" Douglass asked, remembering her own futile attempts at the same when she figured out she was in love with a Yankee at the very worst time in all of history.

"I'm saying that I have no other choice but to fall out of love with Colum. Did he ever tell you the story of the weeping willow?" Ellie sniffled.

"No, but I've got a feeling I'm about to hear it," Douglass said. "Let's go up to your room. I'll get you a cold cloth for your eyes and you can tell me about the willow. Does it have something to do with today or with that willow in my backyard?"

"Both," Ellie said, letting Douglass lead the way to her room.

Indigo heard the commotion and came out of her room in time to follow her sister-in-law, Douglass and her cousin, Ellie into the bedroom. That miserable rebel better hope he hadn't made Ellie cry or Indigo was going to give him a royal piece of her mind. She'd tried really hard to be civil since Christmas but that was only because Ellie had been so happy. That and the fact that she'd given Thomas Brewster permission to come calling on her. He'd said that next

Sunday he'd be around in the afternoon to take her for a ride and maybe she'd show him the new house he'd been hearing so much about. She'd show them all that she could have a beau and one that didn't come from Texas, neither. Ellie would do well to flirt a little with Charlie Brewster. He might not be as handsome as that Texan but he was a good solid man. Owned the general store and lost an eye during the war. The patch made his chubby little face look almost dashing, if Indigo said so herself.

"So what's the problem in here?" she asked.

"Ellie is going to fall out of love with Colum," Douglass wrung cold water from a cloth she'd dipped in the white wash basin.

"Well, praise to the good Lord above. I shall drop down on my knees and give thanks until I have calluses on them. Don't tell me miracles don't still happen. So what did the rascal do? Show you his true colors?" Indigo said.

"Don't you say one mean word about him," Ellie threw the rag from her eyes and dared Indigo to even open her mouth with a glare meant to fry any hateful words before they could escape.

"He made you cry," Indigo snapped, sitting down on the edge of the bed.

"No, he did not make me cry," Ellie said. "I made me cry. I told him the courting was over. He didn't break it off. I did. He's leaving for Texas in six weeks, and I can't go on with the courting, knowing the end is coming. I decided this morning that I would end it today and get it over with."

"Good," Indigo said. "Shows you've got some sense. Tommy Brewster is coming to see me next Sunday. We're taking a drive and I'm showing him the new house. He's dying to see what all the talk is about. I'll just tell him to bring Charlie and we can make it a foursome. That will take your mind off that Rebel."

"Don't you dare," Ellie hissed. "I've no interest whatso-ever in Charlie Brewster."

Douglass smiled. Falling out of love didn't always happen on self-will. She was living proof.

"I was just trying to help," Indigo pouted. "When your favorite kitten dies, you go out and get another one."

"This is a little more than a dead cat," Ellie said. "I don't want anyone to come courting me. It's going to take years to get over this. He told me the story of why the weeping willow weeps. It's so sad but it's just like the two of us." She began to tell the tale of Patrick and Colleen in a voice so soft Douglass and Indigo had to lean forward to hear her. Every now and again, she'd stop and let the sobs wrack her body, then she'd go on. She had to tell it from start to finish. Telling the story might bring closure to her dead heart. Wasn't that why people had funerals when someone died? The dead person didn't know or care about the hymns, the eulogy or the sermon. It was to bring the finish, the closure to the living. Well, Ellie's heart was dead. She had two women with her at the wake for it. The tale of Patrick and Colleen was the eulogy and the sermon as they buried her poor, broken heart.

"It will take years to get over this," Ellie repeated at the finish of the story.

If you ever do, Douglass thought.

"I think the best thing for us to do is let Ellie lie here quietly," Douglass said. "She needs some thinking time."

"She could shovel manure," Indigo said. "Work, work, work. That's what Momma says frees the mind to work things through."

"Tomorrow," Douglass said. "Tomorrow she can work. Today she needs a nice nap and to think."

"And to be alone," Ellie said, her eyes already drooping from the mental exhaustion of the whole ordeal.

She fell asleep minutes after Douglass and Indigo left the room, only to dream of Colum riding a horse out into the sea, where it suddenly sprouted wings to carry him away into the foggy, misty salty smell of the ocean. She crumbled onto the sand and wept in her dream. In reality, fresh tears soaked her pillow.

Douglass found Colum sitting under the willow tree, a haunted look and slick tear stains on his face. She'd never seen her brother cry before. Not when news of their grandfather's death reached them. Not even when he came home with the news that his best friend had died in his arms of a gunshot wound in the war. Colum had the sentiment of the Irish, the passion of the Mexicans and the iron strength of a Texan. He did not cry.

She drew him into her arms, pulling his head down onto her shoulder. Neither of them said a word for a long time. She offered him the strength born of shared blood and love. He took it without hesitation. Clouds covered the sun. Lightning flashed. Thunder roared. Spring was about to be born in a raging storm, yet neither of them moved. When the first big drops of rain fell, he pulled her to her feet and they made their way to the back porch.

Sitting on the swing, out of danger of the rain coming down in solid sheets she held his hand and still kept her silence. He'd speak when he was ready and she'd listen. Even if she had to sit there all day.

"I love her," he said around the lump in his throat, willing himself not to cry in front of his sister. "But she has to take me like I am and not want to change me into what she wants. Unconditional. Texan and all."

"Unconditional is right," Douglass said, remembering her own yearning to go home to Texas with her brothers, but in the end she gave Monroe unconditional love on a silver platter when she figured out she could not live without her heart and it was staying in a little obscure valley in Pennsylvania. Suddenly, Texas, her brothers, her parents, all of whom she loved didn't seem so important.

"The next six weeks are going to be tough. Seeing her every day. Not being able to rush home at dark to tell her about the day," he whispered.

"It will be at that," Douglass said. "Just keep working and the time will go fast. I'll be at the house every day and you can talk to me."

"Thank you, Esmie," he said, using the old pet name he and his brothers called her. "I'm right. Tell me I'm right."

"I'll just tell you to listen to your heart, Colum. It will tell you what is right. It never steers you wrong. Sometimes though you have to listen real close because your own wants and desires get in the way."

Good advice coming from a little sister who'd given him so much fight during their growing up years. He'd listen. He really would. But his heart told him that if Ellie loved him like he loved her she'd be more than willing to leave her home and go with him. Douglass had made that sacrifice and it had brought her happiness. Why couldn't Ellie see that?

Chapter Fourteen

Spring came to the mountains in the next six weeks. Colum didn't go to sleep one night and wake up to minty green leaves on the scrub ash, oaks and even the willow tree in Douglass's backyard. It came about gradually, as gently as the spring breezes and as slowly as Colum's cautious heart brought him around to recognize the fondness he'd begun to have for Love's Valley. Winter was brutal in that part of the world, not at all like his mild Texas winters. But spring was just as lovely, and according to Monroe, the summers mild. Still, even with wild spring flowers painting the countryside in delicate colors, and the joy in his heart at seeing the bitter winter end, he had no reason, other than his sister, to stay.

The house was finished. Extra hands had been hired to put in the final touches so Colum could see the end product before he left the next morning. Douglass had insisted on having a small going away party in her new home to send her brother back to Texas in fine style. Somehow the small family-only party extended to include Thomas Brewster, Indigo's new beau, and then Monroe came up with the idea of making it a big barbecue and inviting all the community to an open house. Douglass never batted one black eyelash when she looped her arms around his neck in front of the whole family and agreed that was a lovely idea. He and Colum could pit roast a couple of pigs. They could kill a steer and call in Otis Chilcote to do his magic with the barbecue. All the women could bring a covered dish and there'd be a whole day of games and fun on the lawn, with fireworks at dark to end the day. Granted, the place wasn't furnished except for the dining room and bedroom, but that didn't matter. Folks could still walk through the empty, hollow rooms and see the reality of Douglass's and Monroe's dream.

Friday morning dawned with a full-blown orange sun peeping over the mountain tops to the east. The sky didn't have even a hint of a rain cloud, and though cool, there was the promise of a lovely day. The whole household had been busy all week in preparation for the day's events. Games on the lawns for the children. Food all day for everyone. Quilts on the clotheslines for anyone who forgot to bring theirs to sit on. All the tables covered with snowy white tablecloths, and benches from the bunkhouse arranged under the shade of trees.

The first wagons appeared at the end of the lane at just past ten o'clock. From then on it was a steady stream, the yard filling up before noon when dinner was served. Ellie and Douglass both kept busy smiling, visiting, giving tours of the grounds, pointing out where the gardens would be another year. Colum helped Otis with the barbecue, giving a bit of advice cautiously here and there about how they did things in Texas. Otis, a gray-haired gentleman, who'd seen more in his lifetime than the aftereffects of a brutish war, listened intently and added a bit more brown sugar to the barbecue sauce recipe he kept secret.

"I hear you're leaving on the noon coach tomorrow," Tommy Brewster said, finding a place to watch the process, his mouth watering at the prospect of a hunk of good barbecued rib.

"That's the plan," Colum said.

"That'll make Indigo happy," Tommy said with a sly grin.

"I guess that's a good thing," Colum said.

"It is from my standpoint," Tommy told him. "I decided when I first met you I wasn't going to like you one bit. Saw a bunch of your kind in the war. Hotheaded Mexicans. Stubborn as a mule. And then Irish, too. Lord, what a combination. But I've decided it was good for you to be here these past months. Good for us in this area to see the house going up and all you've done. Kind of like . . ." he was at a loss for words.

"I appreciate it, Tommy," Colum clapped a hand on his shoulder. "I understand. I sure enough didn't want to come back this way so soon after the war, but my folks sent me to bring that wild sister of mine back home. Guess Indigo told you that story?"

"She sure did. Douglass sure is a pretty woman, though. I can't fault Monroe for falling in love with her. Seems like the wrongest time this side of eternity for a Yank and a Rebel to marry up, but it 'pears like they're making a go of it. Heard you and Ellie was courting there for a while," Tommy said.

"We were, but things didn't work out," Colum said, surprised that admitting it right out loud on that lovely spring day brought a lump in his throat the size of an osage orange.

"That's what Indigo said. She was bound and determined I'd bring Charlie out here to court her, but Charlie ain't got eyes for Ellie Hamilton. He's had his heart set on Abbie Garber since they was barely out of diapers. She married another feller while Charlie and me was gone, but he got killed during the last days of the war. Charlie is just waiting for the proper mourning to be over before he declares his intentions. Who knows, he might even find a quilt to sit on with her at this party," Tommy said.

Colum nodded, not trusting his voice or his temper. How dare that smart mouthed Indigo attempt to undermine him. She had no right to play matchmaker with Ellie so soon after the ordeal with Oscar Wright. For that matter, so soon after their courtship had ended.

"Well, there she is, giving me some mean looks for even talking to you, but before you leave I just wanted to let you know that we don't all of us hate you," Tommy said. "Some of us don't hold to the bitterness of the war like others."

"Thank you," Colum said. "Now if you've a mind to keep courting Indigo, I'd advise you to sashay over that way and get away from me. As it is, you're probably already in trouble."

"I stay in trouble with that woman," Tommy laughed. "She's the opposite of . . ." his voice trailed off again as he blushed scarlet. "Never mind that comment. She'll keep me on my toes, I'm sure."

"That's one area we're in complete agreement on," Colum said, grabbing up a basting mop from a bucket and giving the turning steer another thick coat of a wonderful smelling barbecue sauce.

"So Ellie ain't interested in Charlie Brewster and Charlie is still pining for Abbie Garber?" Otis chuckled. "Wars come and go, but love sure keeps us entertained, now don't it? Us men can talk about battles we fought all day long, but when the sun goes down at night, them battles sure don't keep us warm, now do they? No, sir. It's the love of a good woman keeps us, ain't it?"

Colum didn't know if he was supposed to answer or listen. He chose to do the latter, nodding in agreement.

"Well, now I'll tell you something, Texas. You boys fought for what you thought was right. My boys fought for what they figured was right. Lost two sons in that war. Neither one of them was shot. Brought their bodies home to me to bury up in the Brethren Cemetery. Died of the pneumonia, they did, but they might not have got it if they'd been at home sleeping in a warm bed. I ain't begrudgin' my loss. They was grown men and they made their choice to go fight. I ain't got nothing to hang my head over. But lookin' at you here today, somehow I figured out I ain't been as forgivin' as I thought I was, because there's resentment in my heart about you bein' alive and them being dead. My preacher talked on something called absolution last Sunday. He said God forgives us all the way. Just flat out absolves our sins and we need to be forgiving like that. I guess I ain't God. It's something I'll have to work on for a long time. Maybe that's why I'm making this steer edible today instead of sweeping up the streets of Glory. God knows I've still got some work to do in my heart," Otis said.

"Maybe we all do," Colum said, wondering what the man had been skirting around saying.

"I can finish this up, son," Otis said. "You go on and pay a little attention to your sister and Miss Ellie. It's your last day with them both. Douglass, now ain't that a strange name for a woman? Anyway, she's going to miss you right sorely. She ain't really been without family around her yet and it ain't going to be an easy time for her. And Ellie, well, that little lady has got some hard days ahead of her, too."

"You want to tell me more about why you think that?" Colum asked.

"Not me. I don't talk much. Ask anyone about town. Otis is a man of few words," he said with a deep chuckle. "You go figure it out for yourself. You can't do that, then you wouldn't listen to me no how."

Ellie watched him saunter across the lawn, rolling his shirt sleeves down on the way. A bit of barbecue sauce stained the pocket on the front, but it only added to the allure. A working man, he'd reek of the smell of roasting steer and the soap he'd used that morning to shave. Emotions stirred in her that she didn't want to deal with that day. The taste of loneliness when she couldn't even look at him after tomorrow. The desolate ache of fingertips longing to reach out and brush back the forelock of jet black hair on his forehead. Passion filled her breast. A feeling she had no experience coping with, but even Ellie was wise enough to know passion without total love was as short-lived as a summer butterfly. She'd endured the scorn of Oscar, the waggling of tongues that said so much more had gone on in that cabin, the past miserable six weeks. She could well endure him being gone.

"Pigs are ready to serve," Monroe said as Colum joined the family behind one of the tables. "Charlie Brewster has agreed to carve them over there at the pits. Are we ready to make our welcome, then?"

Douglass tiptoed and kissed him full on the mouth, not caring that the whole of southern Huntingdon County was watching. "We're ready, darlin'," she whispered. "And tonight we sleep in our house, all alone, for the first time. So make sure these people know the party is over at dark."

"You are a Mexican hussy," he whispered back.

"And you love every bit of this hussy," she giggled.

"If I could have your attention," Monroe shouted. "We'd like to welcome you all to our new home and to Love's Valley. They've given me the signal that the pork is roasted to perfection and the steer also, so after Father John says a dinner grace for us we'll begin to eat. Stay around as long as you can and eat as much as you like. We'll end the whole day with fireworks right at dark. For those of you who want to go before dark, we'll understand. For those who want to stay, we're glad to have you. Now Father John."

Grace was short. Father John had spent the morning sucking up the aroma of roasting pigs and barbecue just like everyone else. He said, "Amen," and reached for the first plate all in the same breath.

"So shall I bring your plate?" Ellie asked Colum then wanted to bite her tongue off. Sweet Jesus, what was she thinking? Everyone would see her waiting on him and suppose that they were engaged. There wouldn't be an eligible bachelor in the whole area who'd come sniffing around the back door. *Well, that might be a blessing,* her conscience chided. *You said you wouldn't be ready for such shenanigans for years, so this would fix it up right for you.*

"I would like that very much," Colum said, sitting down

beside Monroe at the table. "Seems strange to look up there and see the house all finished. It'll take a while to fill it up with furniture, though. Who's going to build most of it for you?"

"Douglass was hoping to coerce you into staying around, or maybe coming back for the winter again. You could go home to Texas and then come back during the slow months. Or else, after she begs and cries, you could go home to Texas, build whatever you could in the slow months down there and I'll send a crew from town to bring it all the way here on the back of draft wagons," Monroe said.

"You'd do that? Why?" Colum asked.

"I want sturdy things in that house but most of all I want to make Douglass as happy as she's made me. I never told you or anyone else this, but I'd decided to never trust my heart to anyone on the very day I found her sitting in the middle of the road. I'd been through the whole war and I don't have to tell you what I saw because you were there and saw it, too. Only from the other side. But it does not matter which side we were looking at. Rotting human flesh, broken bones, amputated limbs, dysentery, death. It all smells and looks the same whether it's wearing a blue uniform or a gray one. I was sick of emotions. Sick of loneliness. Sick of it all. I just wanted to come home to Love's Valley and feel nothing. But Douglass Sullivan woke me up right fast and hard. She stirred up my heart like it was a bowl of mush and she had a big wooden spoon. One minute I wanted to wring her pretty neck. The next I entertained kissing her. I didn't know whether to cuss like a soldier or go blind. Finally, I just shut one eye and said a few choice words. By the time you all arrived on the scene I was madly in love with her and no matter how hard I tried, I couldn't fall out of love with the hussy. No offense meant with the word. It's what I call her in private. That and her Irish majesty, since she thought she was absolutely the queen of the whole Confederacy when I rescued her. I'm rambling on and on and here come the women with platters of food for us, but the bottom line is if she wants furniture you build then she'll have it."

"Thank you," Colum said. "I'll see what I can work out."

"I could only carry one platter so we'll share," Douglass said, setting the dish between her and Monroe.

"I see you managed two," Colum raised a dark eyebrow at Ellie, and without thinking, reached up to brush an errant strand of blond hair back behind her ear toward the snug bun at the nape of her neck.

"Of course, I'm not expecting a baby so my balance is better," Ellie said, high color filling her cheeks. Horse manure on a shingle, she didn't have a bit of social grace in her body that day. Ladies never mentioned things like that before menfolks. Not even their favorite cousins, fathers or brothers. It was barely acceptable to talk about it in the privacy of a parlor full of women.

"I'm glad to know that," Monroe laughed. "Sit down here, Ellie, between me and Colum. We saved you a seat."

That did it! If she sat there, they might as well be courting again. She couldn't not sit down after Monroe had saved her a seat. So she sat, and nibbled around the edges of a plate laden high with food. Her stomach was nothing more than a quivering mass of jelly and her heart was even worse. Every time her shoulder brushed against Colum's the jolt of desire romping through her veins set her on fire. She chewed. She swallowed. Nothing had flavor.

After an hour of agony sitting beside him she finally excused herself to go help Aunt Laura in the kitchen where the clean up was taking place. The minute she was out of sight an empty vacuum filled Colum's breast. The time she'd been there, he was alive again. His pulse raced. His heart thumped out a rhythm that sounded like a Celtic love song in his ears. Her smooth, sweet voice was like fine Texas bourbon laced with honey, and soothed his soul. Then there was nothing.

"You sure you don't want to stay around and make furniture for me all summer? I'll beg," Douglass asked.

"I don't think I could stand it," Colum whispered. "No, *querida,* I'm going home tomorrow and try to reconstruct my old sentimental Irish heart, but the first thing I'll make is a cradle for my new niece or nephew and I'll send it along with Momma when she comes for the summer. Otis brought along a letter this morning that I've been keeping to surprise you with. Momma and Flannon are planning to be here about the time the baby is due. I'm telling you so you'll have something to look forward to. Just a few more months and more family will be here to keep you company. She says they'll leave at the end of the summer in case there's another early winter. Flannon says he's not staying in this forsaken place during a snowstorm," Colum held the letter out to her.

"Oh Monroe," she wiped the back of her hand across her eyes. "Can you believe it? My Momma is coming for the birth. I can hardly wait for her to see our new home and Love's Valley. And Flannon, too. Please Colum, tell me you'll come back with them?"

"No, ma'am, when you wave good-bye to me at the station tomorrow I'll not be back for a long time. Next time you see this scarred face in Love's Valley, there'll be a train to bring me the whole way and you'll have enough kids to fill up that house," he said.

Douglass's chin quivered.

"Won't work, little sister," Colum said. "Might bring Monroe to his knees, but not this old Texan."

"You're mean and hateful," Douglass got control of her chin immediately. "There's all that family back there to keep each other company and you won't even stay here until Momma gets here? You could build my cradle right here on the place, then go home with them in the fall."

"Could but ain't goin' to," he said. "Now before a real Sullivan family fight starts up, I'm going to go take one more look at that house. Besides, I understand both of Monroe's brothers are coming home this summer, too. That'll give you lots of family around you."

Ellie had slipped in the front door and up the stairs. She'd hide away in one of the bedrooms. Aunt Laura, who was supervising the clean up in the new kitchen, would think she was still outside. Douglass, Indigo and the rest of the people would think she was inside helping Aunt Laura. She needed, had to have, a few moments of time alone to collect her feelings. To still her shaking limbs and quell the distress in her heart. She slipped up the wide slightly curved staircase to the upper floor and closed one of the empty bedroom doors behind her. She slid down the backside of the door, the full skirt of her new pale blue calico dress fanning out around her like a billowing cloud. She'd put her face in her hands when she felt the presence of someone else in the room.

"So you've had enough of the crowd, too?" Fred asked. "I wasn't going to come out here today, seeing as how I was fired on butchering day, but I decided that I wanted to see this house all finished, so I came. But I'm not socializing or eating Hamilton food. No, sir. I've just come to see the house and now I'm going home. Soon as you get away from that door."

Ellie pushed a hand down in the fabric of her skirt and attempted to stand, but got off balance when the heel of her shoe got caught up in her petticoat. She was half way up and falling back down when Fred caught her in his strong arms and hauled her to her feet. Not one spark jumped when his hands touched hers. Just when she had recovered her footing, scarcely a yard inside the door, it swung open and slung her back into Fred's arms again.

Colum stood in the open doorway, surprise written on his face. So that's the way it was? She'd already fallen for someone else. *One thing for sure, it'll make leaving a lot easier,* he thought as he stood there in a perfectly still tableau.

"This is not what it looks like. Fred caught me when I started to fall," Ellie pushed away from Fred's arms, her nose snarling at the smell of the man. Whiskey and sweat combined in a not so savory mixture.

"It's none of my business," Colum said.

"I'm just leaving," Fred said. "Didn't come for the social-izing. Came to see the house, not any of you. I ain't got to explain nothing," he said and was down the stairs before either Colum or Ellie could collect their thoughts.

"Good day, then. I'm sorry I burst in on you and your *a ghra* that way. Didn't know you'd come away up here for a rendezvous. You should tell Monroe that you've forgiven Fred for his hasty decision last winter. Monroe might let him stay for the fireworks then you can kiss him good-bye," Colum said coldly.

"Maybe I will," Ellie retorted. "If I do or don't it's not one bit of your business."

"And I'm right glad it's not," Colum nodded, ice dripping from his tone and shooting from his eyes.

"Me, too," Ellie poked him in the chest, ignoring the burn-ing in her fingertips as she did so. "You don't have any say-so in what I do or don't do. Who I choose to be friends with or not. So go on back to your precious Texas, Colum."

"Did I really throw you into his arms with that door?" Colum grinned at her spunk and anger, all the anger gone from him when the realization finally hit him between the eyes about what had really happened. Holy Smoke, Ellie had more sense than to deliberately fall into the arms of a man like Fred. Even slick-talking Oscar was by far more to look at than Fred.

His change of heart did nothing more than fire her rage up even hotter.

"I don't owe you an explanation," she said.

"Can't imagine you kissing a mouth that had snuff juice dried up all around it," he said. "Can't imagine you kissing anything but my mouth," he said, catching her arms and pinning her to his chest. Their hearts beat in unison. The world stood still and the room began to spin around Ellie so fast she thought she'd faint. He tipped her chin back and savored the kiss for a long, long time. It would be the last one, he had no doubt, and the memory of it would have to last him a lifetime.

Ellie was glad he held her tightly or her weak knees would have failed her. She leaned into the kiss, tasting the sweet barbecue and the masculinity that was just plain Colum. If only passion could build love, they'd never part. But it couldn't and when she stepped out of his embrace it was with new purpose.

"Your imagination isn't so good. Not for an Irishman who tells pretty stories about fairies and willow trees," she said. "Because I'll kiss whoever I want. Good-bye, Colum." She swept her skirts aside and head held high, went down the stairs and out the back door to sit beneath the willow tree— alone.

Chapter Fifteen

They rode in silence that foggy morning. Douglass and Ellie in the back of the covered buggy. Colum and Monroe in the front. Ellie and her big mouth had gotten her into the predicament of seeing Colum off. She'd casually mentioned at the breakfast table that she had some banking to do that week if Monroe was going into town anytime soon. Douglass jumped on the idea like flies on a fresh cow chip. Ellie could just go with them that very day since they were both going to town to take Colum to the stage station. Ellie had stammered and stuttered but in the end there was nothing to do but go with them.

Though silent, Douglass held in her laughter. Just let them have to part at the stage and see how they liked that. She remembered her own feelings the morning she and her two brothers were getting in the buggy to leave Love's Valley. The very place she hated with all her might and vigor suddenly became the place she loved because that's where Monroe lived. She remembered the heavy heart she dragged across the porch that morning and felt sorry for Ellie. But Douglass had done all she could do at that point. Either they would be adults and face the fact they were in love or they'd have to spend some time apart figuring it out. Either way,

Douglass had a bet going with Monroe that Colum would be back before the baby was born. She wouldn't be surprised if he didn't even make it all the way back to Texas before he figured out he couldn't live without a heart. Strange, how two Texans who loved their state, had come to care so much about an obscure little valley in south central Pennsylvania.

Monroe began to whistle as they traveled down the mountainside. A slow mournful tune he hoped wrung tears from both Ellie and Colum's hearts. That they belonged together was plain to everyone but the two of them. Stubborn. That's what they were. But then it ran in both their bloodlines. No one in the whole United States of America could be more stubborn than a Hamilton. He, Henry Rueben and Harry Reed had all got double doses of bull-headedness. Yes, sir, the Hamiltons had that quality roped and branded. And right behind them in the contest of who had the most mulishness stood the Sullivans. Heaven help the world if his firstborn got blessed with both his and Douglass's hard heads. To Monroe's notion, Ellie and Sullivan deserved the misery they were wallowing in. Either one of them were capable of opening their hearts and mouths and this could be over. It didn't matter if they went to Texas or stayed in Pennsylvania. As long as they were together. He wouldn't relish the idea of his cousin going to Texas but he'd rather see her do that than stay in Love's Valley and be miserable.

Ellie kept her eyes ahead, boring holes in Colum's back. How could she have let herself fall in love with him? And why couldn't she simply fall out of love the same way? It boggled the brain, that's what it did. She'd never been in love with Oscar, now that she could look back with perfect hindsight. He'd been a passing fancy, maybe even a last ditch effort against being an old maid. Pride was all that kept Elspeth Hamilton from demanding that Monroe stop the carriage so she could fall at Colum's feet and beg him to take her to Texas with him.

Holy mother of Jesus, had she really just thought such a thing? she asked herself, frowning and chewing on her thumbnail at the same time. If she didn't quit thinking such blasphemous words, her mother was truly going to raise up out of the grave and chastise her. What would her mother or father think of Colum? An Irishman at heart. Mexican by birth. Rebel to boot. What a combination. The nearer they got to Shirleysburg, the more she dreaded seeing him go. A week chained to a cabin wall had only filled her with rage. But knowing that Colum would perhaps never return chilled her to the bone. She shivered against emptiness so painful that the only sound in it was a haunting echo of the loneliness crying out in its wake. Still she couldn't voice the words in her heart.

The shroud of quietness, saving for the sound of Monroe's whistling, lay like a thick blanket on Colum's shoulders. Why had he kissed her yesterday in the house? It just made the leaving much harder. If he wasn't so blasted hardheaded, he'd tell her so, too. But that wasn't the way of a Sullivan. No sir, they were men's men and they didn't grovel in front of women. 'Twas the wrong thing, for sure, that he was about to do, yet he had no control over it. He didn't want to leave Love's Valley that fine morning. And now, in the distance, down the main street of Shirleysburg, he could hear the faint wailing of the banshee. She was coming to warn an Irish family that one of theirs was about to die, coming to collect the soul and take it to live in the fairy rafts beneath the land. He strained his ears and hoped there were other Irish in the community although he'd not seen a one. To be sure, the banshee wouldn't have come all the way into Yankee territory to warn him that one of his own was about to leave this world. Most likely she was mourning for his own heartache. But the silver-haired fairies who warned of upcoming fatalities did not wail over broken hearts. He shivered, fought back the urge to cross himself and sent up a prayer that Douglass would be kept safe in this strange, harsh land he'd come to love.

Love! He didn't love this land. Far from it. He despised the winter. *Ah, but to enjoy a glorious spring like this, one must experience the winter,* his Irish father's voice was as clear as if it was speaking to him from the next room. *And your feeling for the lovely lass was like the winter. Cold. Unforgiving. In the past months it's bloomed into something as delicate and lovely as the flowers of spring. You're making a mistake Colum Eduardo. Did you think I didn't have a battle leaving my green, fair Ireland for the wilds of Texas? If she's worth your love, she's worth fighting for, worth leaving all behind to wake up beside her each morning. I would have given my wealth to a beggar on the street if that's what it took to have your mother.*

Now where did all that come from? Colum wondered, as the carriage stopped in front of the bank.

"Colum, if you'll go with Ellie into the bank, I'll escort Douglass to the general store for the fabric she needs. Baby clothing has now become the order of the day," Monroe chuckled. "We will meet you at the stage station in half an hour. It leaves promptly at noon so don't be late. Ellie's business shouldn't take more than ten minutes."

"I can take care of it alone," Ellie said, removing her gloves and tucking them into the reticule hanging by a drawstring on her arm. She'd have to remember to give the little gun back to Colum, but she would wait until the last minute. Returning it was symbolic of all ties being broken and she wasn't quite ready for that. Just another half an hour to let the little gold derringer lay as heavy in her purse as her heart in her chest.

"I don't mind," Colum held up his hands to help her out of the carriage. Sparks flew around them so brilliantly, it rivaled the fireworks show from the night before.

She swept her skirt tail to one side to walk up the three steps to the sidewalk in front of the bank and waited for him to open the door for her. So caught up in her own feelings, she was halfway inside the bank, on the way to the teller's window when she realized something wasn't right.

"Shut the door, Rebel," a familiar voice came from the dark shadows of one side of the bank. "And lock it behind you. Now ain't this the nicest little surprise ever?"

Ellie whipped around to find Oscar Wright no more than two feet from her. Her nostrils flared in disgust. "What are you doing here?" she demanded in a shrill voice.

"Why, honey, I'm robbing this bank. It's the cake and you are the icing on it. Who'd a thought this was the day I'd take care of you and this bank? Mr. Sullivan, you take that gun out of its holster right easy. Butt first and put it on the floor," Oscar reached out and grabbed a handful of hair, dragging Ellie to his side with it, yet not taking his eyes off Colum.

"Let her go. Let her walk out of here and sit in the carriage. You have my word she won't make a sound until you're finished and gone," Colum said calmly as he laid his Colt on the floor and kicked it out of the way.

"Now wouldn't that be kicking the gods in the face?" Oscar laughed in his face.

There were three of them standing shoulder to shoulder, guns drawn, bags of money in Turley and Alvie's hands. The bank teller and owner were tied to chairs and gagged. Colum could take out one of them with the knife he had hidden inside a sheath in the waistband of his trousers, but in doing so they might shoot Ellie.

"She's done walked in here just when we were leaving. I reckon that means the gods intend for me to have her yet. She's the cause I'm on the run, robbing banks and staying a step ahead of the law, so she can provide me and the boys with a little sport before I kill her," Oscar pulled her toward the door with him.

"I will not," she whispered.

"Oh, honey, you will," Oscar squeezed her so hard she feared she'd loose her breath.

Ellie set her heels and went limp. Colum figured she'd fainted and prayed that was the case since they'd probably just kick her aside rather than try to carry that much dead weight with them. He deftly fingered the knife, biding his time, trying to decide which head to plant the sharp doubled-edged knife into.

While Ellie let out all the air from her lungs and pretended to give way to a case of the vapors, she dug around in the little reticule for the derringer. When she had it firmly in her hand, she crossed her hand under her breast, raised her arm slightly and shoved it into Oscar's chest. She didn't try to sweet talk him into letting her go. She didn't utter a word. She simply pulled the trigger twice.

At the sound of the gun going off, Colum jerked the knife from its sheath and drew back to throw it. But before it could leave his hands both Turley and Alvie turned their guns on Ellie. Both fired, and all four people dropped in a bloody heap on the bank floor, bags of money flying into the air. Bills rained down on the bank owner and the teller, floating from the ceiling even as spirits left dead bodies and ascended toward that judgment hall in the sky.

When the firing stopped and the smoke settled, Colum dropped to his knees. Ellie was dead by the hands of Oscar Wright after all. He'd rescued her for nothing. Fallen in love with her for naught. His heart fell to his feet and lay there on the floor amongst all the money in a shattered jumble of jagged pieces that would never fit back together. Colum had waited too late to beg her to go to Texas with him. He waited too late to offer to stay in Love's Valley with her. Like Patrick and Colleen they were star crossed lovers and he'd never have anything but emptiness this side of eternity.

He put his head in his hands, ignoring the whimpers of the gagged men. He shut his eyes and a thousand visions danced there—all of Ellie. In that cabin with shackles on her legs. Bruises on her body from that sorry excuse for a man. In the Leine-and-Brat with a poncho over it. The confident look on her face when she kissed him on Christmas and said she was going to court him. Sweet memories, sweet memories. The banshee had been warning him after all. It was he who heard the wailing so he should have known it would be the love of his life who was about to be taken.

He opened his eyes and crawled on his hands and knees to the bodies where blood ran in puddles onto the floor. He gathered Ellie into his arms, not even noticing the warm blood that covered his hands. He stood up with her tucked against his chest. Leaving three dead men in the grotesque way they'd fallen and two with veins about to burst in their heads as they tried in vain to get his attention, he carried his *a ghra* out the door and down the street to the doctor's office.

"Don't be dead," he whispered, hoping against the odds that the bullets had only grazed her and hadn't hit any vital organs.

"What happened?" Monroe came running toward him.

"Oscar robbed the bank. Ellie's been shot and I think she's dead," Colum didn't even try to hide the tears streaming down his cheeks.

"No, I'm not," she whispered in a strange voice that didn't sound anything like hers to her aching ears. "I'm not shot, but I'm scared senseless. When those two pointed guns at me, I really did faint. You sound like you are talking out of the end of a barrel though."

Colum sat down in the middle of the sidewalk with her in his lap, checking her arms, her neck, her body, but found no holes. Just blood, which had evidently come from the men and not her at all.

"Oh, *a ghra,*" he moaned, burying his face in her hair. "I love you. I'll stay. I'll beg you to go with me. I can't live without you."

"I'll go with you," she said. "Or I'll beg you to stay with me here in Love's Valley, but please don't go today, Colum. When I fainted, all I could think was that I'd be making the biggest mistake of my life if I told you good-bye." She buried her face in his chest and let her own tears of absolution mix with his. A heart full of love had no place for bitterness, revenge, the holding of grudges.

"I suppose we'd best go get the sheriff," Monroe said, looking up to see Douglass hurrying down the street. Hadn't he told her to stay in the general store? Lord, that woman was going to be the death of him.

"Please do," Ellie shouted above the ringing in her head. "I'll wait right here with Colum."

Monroe intercepted Douglass in front of the bank and turned her around to go with him to the sheriff's office. "Let them be. Ellie's had a fright, but I think maybe you're going to win the bet, if you'll just leave them alone. They're already promising each other the moon and stars."

"Will you really stay?" Ellie asked.

"Will you really go?" Colum asked back.

"I'd go anywhere if you'll have me," Ellie said.

"Is that a proposal I hear from your pretty lips?" Colum asked.

"It is," Ellie snuggled down tighter. "Is Oscar dead?"

"He is," Colum wrapped his arms around her even tighter.

"I'm glad, and it's not going to make me a raving lunatic that I shot him. When he fell, he pulled me with him. I saw both of those men draw and fire toward me. I think they killed each other," she said.

"I believe you're right," Colum let her work it out in her own way. He'd wasn't going anywhere today except back home . . . home to Love's Valley where his heart had shown him he belonged, and where the banshee decided to give him a second chance.

"Are you going to marry me?" She leaned back to study his face. She ran her fingertips across his brow to erase the worry wrinkles, then touched the scar where she'd marked him on the first day she met him.

"Yes, ma'am, I reckon I am, soon as you say the magic words," he said.

"That would be please?" she asked.

"No, that would be those three words I need to hear," he said.

"I love you? Well, that's a given. I don't propose to men I don't love," she whispered as the crowd began to draw around them.

"Is she hurt?" Charlie was the first to reach their sides.

"No, just scared. You'll find the bank robbers dead and the teller and owner both tied up. I expect they'd be right glad to have you release them," Colum said, still not moving from the sitting position.

"Now you tell me," she said.

"I love you," he said just barely below a full-fledged shout. "I love you, Ellie Hamilton and I'm askin' you to marry me."

Snickers and whoops sounded up and down the sidewalk.

"Yes," she said loudly. "Yes, Colum Sullivan I will gladly marry you! This afternoon at two o'clock in the living room of Douglass and Monroe's new house."

Colum was speechless. "Today?"

"Yes, today, so that you don't change your mind. Tomorrow we'll go to Texas," she yelled.

"Tomorrow we'll work on the plans for a house on up the road from Douglass and Monroe," he said. "We'll live in Love's Valley, *a ghra,* where we belong."

"Oh, Colum, you've just made me the happiest woman in all the world," she drew his lips down to hers.

Later that night she slipped between the sheets and snuggled into her new husband's arms. "You can change your mind. I won't hold you to that promise to stay here. We can make our home wherever you want. I'm willing to go to Texas with you, Colum. What you said in Shirleysburg was said in the aftermath of a terrible fright."

"Hush, *querida,*" he put his fingers on her lips. "It was

said from the heart. Love's Valley is where we will make our home and raise our house full of ornery children."

"I want lots of children. I was an only child and the only kids I had to play with were my Hamilton cousins," she trailed kisses across his face and neck.

"I shall be most happy to fulfill your dreams," he grinned, "now blow out that candle, please *querida*."

"With pleasure," she said and with one puff of breath sent the room into darkness. But the warm love glowing inside their hearts would keep their world lit up forever.